D1152875

THE NANNY
AND THE CEO

THE NANNY AND THE CEO

BY

REBECCA WINTERS

First published in Great Britain 2011
by Mills & Boon, an imprint of Harlequin (UK) Limited,
Large Print edition 2011
Eton House, 18-24 Paradise Road,
Richmond, Surrey TW9 1SR

© Rebecca Winters 2011

ISBN: 978 0 263 22204 3

Harlequin (UK) policy is to use papers that are natural,
renewable and recyclable products and made from
wood grown in sustainable forests. The logging and
manufacturing process conform to the legal environmental
regulations of the country of origin.

Printed and bound in Great Britain
by CPI Antony Rowe, Chippenham, Wiltshire

117076541 CSH 09/11

To my wonderful parents,
who made life wonderful all the time
and gave me every opportunity to find my life,
just as the Mother Superior at the convent
helped Maria to find hers.

CHAPTER ONE

"Ms. CHAMBERLAIN? You're next. Second door on the left."

"Thank you."

Reese got up from the chair and walked past the woman at the front desk to reach the hall. At ten o'clock in the morning, the East 59th Street Employment Agency in New York's east side was already packed with people needing a job. She'd asked around and had learned it was one of the most reputable agencies in the city. The place reminded her of her dentist's office filled with patients back home in Nebraska.

She had no idea what one wore for an interview to be a nanny. After changing outfits several times she'd opted for a yellow tailored, short-sleeved blouse and skirt, the kind she'd worn to the initial interview on Wednesday. This was her only callback in three days. If she didn't get hired today, she would have to fly home tomorrow, the last thing she wanted to do.

Her father owned a lumberyard and could always give her a job if she couldn't find anything that suited her, but it wouldn't pay her the kind of money she needed. Worse, she didn't relish the idea of seeing Jeremy again, but it would be inevitable because her ex-fiancé happened to work as a loan officer at the bank where her dad did business. Word would get around she was back.

"Come in, Ms. Chamberlain."

"Hello, again, Mr. Lloyd." He was the man who'd taken her initial application.

"Let me introduce you to Mrs. Tribe. She's the private secretary to a Mr. Nicholas Wainwright here in New York and has been looking for the right nanny for her employer. I'll leave you two alone for a few minutes."

The smart-looking brunette woman wearing a professional business suit was probably in her early fifties. "Please sit down. Reese, is it?"

"Yes."

The other woman cocked her head. "You have

excellent references. From your application it's apparent you're a student and a scholar. Since you're single and have no experience taking care of other people's children, why did you apply to be a nanny?"

Reese could lie, but she had a feeling this woman would see right through her. "I need to earn as much money as possible this summer so I can stay in school until graduation. My academic scholarship doesn't cover housing and food. Even those of us born in fly-over-country have heard a nanny's job in New York can pay very well, so I thought I'd try for a position." Hopefully that explanation was frank enough for her.

"Taking care of children is exceptionally hard work. I know because I raised two of my own."

Reese smiled. "I've never been married, but I'm the oldest in the family of six children and did a lot of babysitting over the years. I was fourteen when my youngest sister was born. My mother had to stay in bed, so I helped with the baby. It was like playing house. My sister was adorable and I loved it. But," she said as she sighed, "that was twelve years ago. Still, taking care of children is like learning to tie your shoes, don't you think? Once you've figured it out, you never forget."

The other woman eyed her shrewdly while she nodded. "I agree."

"How many children do they have?" *Please don't let the number be more than three.* Although Reese wouldn't turn it down if the money was good enough.

"Mr. Wainwright is a widower with a ten-week-old baby boy named Jamie."

The news concerning the circumstances came as a sobering revelation to Reese. She'd assumed she might end up working for a couple with several children, that is if she were ever offered a job. "Then he's still grieving for his wife." She shook her head. "How sad for him and his little boy, who'll never know his mother."

Reese got a swelling in her throat just thinking of her own wonderful mom still remarkably young and vital, probably the same age as Mrs. Tribe.

"It's a tragic loss for both of them. Mr. Wainwright has arranged for a nanny who's been with another family to start working for him, but she can't come until September. Because you only wanted summer work, that's one of the reasons I was interested in your application."

One of the reasons? She'd aroused Reese's curiosity. "What were the others?"

"You didn't name an unrealistic salary. Finally, one of your professors at Wharton told me you've been on full academic scholarship there. Good for you. An opportunity like that only comes to a very elite group of graduate students. It means you're going to have a brilliant career in business one day."

To run her own brokerage firm was Reese's goal for the future. "That's my dream."

The dream that had torn her and Jeremy apart.

Jeremy had been fine about her finishing up her undergraduate work at the University of Nebraska, but the scholarship to Wharton had meant a big move to Pennsylvania. The insinuation that she was too ambitious led to the core of the problem eating at him. Jeremy hadn't wanted a future-executive for a wife. In return

Reese realized she'd had a lucky escape from a future-controlling-husband. Their breakup had been painful at the time, but the hurt was going away. She didn't want him back. Therein lay the proof.

Mrs. Tribe sat back in her chair and studied Reese. "It was my dream, too, but I didn't get the kind of grades I saw on your transcripts. Another of your professors told me he sees a touch of genius in you. I liked hearing that about you."

Reese couldn't imagine which professor that was. "You've made my day."

"Likewise," she murmured, sounding surprised by her own thoughts. "Provided you feel good about the situation after seeing the baby and discussing Mr. Wainwright's expectations of you in that regard, I think you'll do fine for the position. Of course the final decision will be up to him."

Reese could hardly believe she'd gotten this far in the interview. "I don't know how to thank you, Mrs. Tribe. I promise I won't let him, or you, down. Do you have a picture of the baby?"

A frown marred her brow. "I don't, but you'll be meeting him and his father this afternoon.

Where have you been staying since you left Philadelphia?"

"At the Chelsea Star Hotel on West 30th."

"You did say you were available immediately?"

"Yes!" The dormitory bed cost her fifty dollars a night. She couldn't afford to stay in New York after today.

"That's good. If he decides to go with my recommendation and names a fee that's satisfactory to you, then he'll want you to start today."

"What should I wear to the interview? Do I need some kind of uniform? This is completely new to me."

"To both of us," came her honest response. "Wear what you have on. If he has other suggestions, he'll tell you."

"Does he have a pet?"

"As far as I know he's never mentioned one. Are you allergic?"

"No. I just thought if he did, I could pick up some cat or doggie treats at the store. You know. To make friends right off?"

The woman smiled. "I like the way you think, Ms. Chamberlain."

"Of course the baby's going to be another story," Reese murmured. "After having his daddy's exclusive attention, it will take time to win him around."

Mrs. Tribe paused before speaking. "Actually, since his birth, he's been looked after by his maternal grandparents."

"Are they still living with Mr. Wainwright?"

"No. The Hirsts live in White Plains. An hour away in heavy traffic."

So did that mean he hadn't been with his son for the last couple of months? No…that couldn't be right. Now that he was getting a nanny, they'd probably just left to go back home.

"I see. Does Jamie have paternal grandparents, too?"

"Yes. At the moment they're away on a trip," came the vague response.

Reese came from a large family. Both sets of grandparents were still alive and always around. She had seven aunts and uncles. Last count there were twenty-eight cousins. With her siblings, including the next oldest, Carrie, who was married and had two children under three, that brought the number to thirty-four. She wondered if her employer had any brothers and sisters or other family.

"You've been with Mr. Wainwright a long time. Is there anything of importance I should know ahead of time?"

"He's punctual."

"I'll remember that." Reese got to her feet. "I won't take any more of your time. Thank you for this opportunity, Mrs. Tribe."

"It's been my pleasure. A limo will be sent for you at one o'clock."

"I'll be waiting outside in front. Oh—one more question. What does Mr. Wainwright do for a living?"

The other woman's eyebrows lifted. "Since you're at Wharton, I thought you might have already made the connection or I would have told you. He's the CEO at Sherborne-Wainwright & Co. on Broadway. Good luck."

"Thank you," Reese murmured in shock.

He was *that* Wainwright?

It was one of the most prestigious brokerage firms in New York, if not *the* top one with roots that went back a couple of hundred years. The revelation stunned her on many levels. Somehow she'd imagined the man who ran the whole thing to be in his late forties or early fifties. It usually took that long to rise to those heights.

Of course it wasn't impossible for him to have a new baby, but she was still surprised. Maybe it had been his second wife he'd lost and she'd been a young mother. No one was exempt from pain in this life.

Nick Wainwright stood at the side of the grave. *In loving memory of Erica Woodward Hirst Wainwright.*

Thirty-two years old was too young to die.

"I'm sorry I neglected you so much it led to our divorce, Erica. Before we separated, I never thought for one moment you might be pregnant with our child, or that you'd lose your life during the delivery. My heart grieves for our little boy who needs his mother. It was your dying wish I raise him, but I feared I wouldn't know how to be a good father to him. That's why I let your parents take care of him this long, but now I'm ready. I swear I'll do everything in my power to be a better father to him than I was a husband to you. If you're listening, I just wanted you to know I vow to keep that promise."

After putting fresh flowers against the head-stone, Nick walked swiftly to the limo waiting for him in the distance. He hadn't been here since the funeral. The visit filled him with sorrow for what had gone wrong, but with the decision made to take Jamie home, it felt right to have come to her grave first.

This early in the morning there was only his chauffeur, Paul, to see his tall, dark lone figure get in the back wearing a pale blue summer suit and tie. As he closed the rear door his eyes flicked to the newest state-of-the-art infant car seat he'd had delivered. Before the morning was out, he'd be taking his ten-week-old boy back to the city with him.

"Let's head over to my in-laws."

His middle-aged driver nodded and started the car. Paul had worked for Nick's dad, back when Nick had been in his early teens. Now that his father was semiretired and Nick had been put in as head of the firm, he'd inherited Paul. Over the years the two of them had become good friends.

Once they left the White Plains cemetery where members of the prominent Hirst family had been buried for the past one hundred and fifty years, he sat back rubbing his hand over his face. In a few minutes there was going to be a scene, but he'd been preparing himself for it.

Prior to the baby's birth, Nick hadn't lived with Erica over the nine months of her pregnancy. Her death had come as a tremendous shock to him. Though he'd allowed her parents to take the baby home from the hospital, he hadn't intended on it lasting for more than several weeks. In that amount of time he'd planned to find live-in help for the baby. Because of his guilt over the way their marriage had fallen apart, he'd let the situation go on too long.

When Nick had phoned the pediatrician in White Plains who'd been called in at the time of delivery, he'd informed Nick that if he hoped to bond with his son, he shouldn't wait any longer to parent him on a full-time basis.

The doctor gave Nick the name of Dr. Hebert Wells, a highly recommended pediatrician who had a clinic on New York's upper west side and could take over Jamie's care. Then he wished him luck.

Following that conversation, Nick had phoned his attorney and explained what he wanted to do. The other man had contacted the Hirsts' attorney to let them know Nick was ready to take over his responsibilities as a father and would be coming for Jamie to take him home.

Erica's parents had wanted Nick to wait until the nanny they'd lined up would be available. They wanted control over the way their only grandchild—a future Hirst who would carry on the family tradition—would be raised. That meant having equal input over everything, the kind of children he associated with and where he would attend school from the beginning through college.

But Nick wasn't willing to wait any longer. Through their attorneys he promised to consult them on certain matters and bring Jamie to White Plains for visits, but deep down he knew nothing he said would reassure them. Time would have to take care of the problem.

Nick's family, who lived on Long Island, wanted control of *their* only grandchild, too. But they were at the family villa in Cannes with friends at the moment, confident Nick would do what had to be done to keep his in-laws pacified.

"Erica's parents seem willing to keep him for now," his mother exclaimed. "It would be better if you let Jamie stay with them for the next year anyway. You can go on visiting him when you have the time. It's the best arrangement under the circumstances."

Nick knew the script by heart. His own parents had already found another suitable woman for Nick to meet when he was ready. They saw nothing wrong in letting Erica's parents oversee Jamie's care, a sort of consolation prize to remove their guilt by association with the son who'd divorced "the catch of the season."

Their attitude came as no surprise to Nick. He'd been an only child, raised in virtual luxury by a whole staff of people other than his own parents. What they never understood was that it had been a lonely life, one that had caused him great pain. He didn't want that for Jamie. But deep down he felt nervous as hell.

Though Nick might have been the whiz kid who'd risen to the top of Sherborne-Wainwright, a two-hundred-year-old family investment brokerage, he didn't quite know what to do with Jamie. The world of a two-and-half-month-old baby was anathema to him.

He'd visited him every Saturday, but was an unwelcome visitor as far as Erica's family was concerned. They had a well-trained, well-vetted staff, plus a private nurse to see to Jamie's every need.

Weather permitting, he would carry the baby outside to the English garden where he could get away from the officious woman in her white uniform. Otherwise Nick remained in the nursery, but he was superfluous in the help department. The staff had everything covered ahead of time. That in itself made it impossible for him to get close to his son.

As the old Georgian colonial estate came into sight and they passed through the outer gate, Nick determined everything was going to change, starting now. He alighted from the back of the limo. "I won't be long, Paul."

The slightly balding family man smiled. "I'm looking forward to seeing him. He's bigger every time we come."

That was the problem. Jamie was changing and growing with each passing day and Nick wasn't here to see it happen. The commuting had to stop so the fathering could begin.

Before he reached the gleaming white front door, Erica's father opened it. Walter had a full head of frosted brown hair and a golfer's physique. Erica's parents were handsome people, but his father-in-law's glowering expression brought out Nick's temper, which he did his best to keep under control.

"Walter?"

"Before I let you in, I want you to know Anne's in a highly emotional state."

"You think I'm not aware of that?"

The older man grimaced. "She asked me to tell yo—"

"I know it by heart, Walter," he broke in. "Though I can't go back and change the past, I intend to do the right thing for our son. I told that to Erica when I stopped at the cemetery a little while ago."

Walter's eyes flickered as if he were surprised by the admission. After a slight hesitation he said, "Come in the dayroom. The nurse has Jamie ready for you."

"Thank you."

After three years of marriage—the last year spent in separation while the divorce was being finalized—his in-law's home was full of ghosts from the past. In the beginning his wedding to Erica had been happy enough. Everyone claimed the lovely Hirst daughter was the catch of the season, but time proved they weren't meant for each other, and she'd spent a lot of her time here rather than the city.

There'd been unmet expectations and disappointments on both sides. The sameness of their existence had become so severe, they'd drifted apart. The last time they'd been intimate, it had been a halfhearted attempt on his part to rekindle what they'd lost, but the spark was gone.

He followed his father-in-law through the house until they came to the dayroom, a contemporary addition that had been constructed after Erica had moved back with them. No doubt to keep her busy with something to do while she waited for the baby to come.

Anne's series of decorators had filled it with pots of flowers and rattan couches covered in bright prints of pink and orange. The floor-to-ceiling windows overlooked several acres of garden and manicured lawns that were green and smooth as velvet.

His mother-in-law sat in one of the chairs, stiff as a piece of petrified wood. Nick's gaze flew to his son, who was lying in the fancy baby carriage. He'd been dressed for travel and was wide-awake.

Nick had no complaints about Jamie's care, but couldn't wait to take him away because he'd be damned if he would allow history to repeat itself for one more day. Nick had been emotionally neglected by his parents. Erica had suffered the same fate though she could never admit it and preferred living in denial.

There'd been a lot of damage done. He wasn't about to commit the same crime where Jamie was concerned.

"Hello, Anne."

She couldn't bring herself to look at him.

Nick walked over to the carriage, still awed by the fact that he was a father, that he and Erica were responsible for Jamie's existence.

The baby had inherited Nick's long, lean body and black hair, but Nick saw hints of Erica's nose and bone structure in his face. She'd been an attractive, slim brunette of medium height like Anne.

"Hi, sport. Remember me?" Nick leaned over and grasped Jamie's tiny hand. One look at Nick and the baby breathed a little faster with excitement. He wrapped his fingers around Nick's index finger. The next thing he knew it went to his mouth, always to the mouth, causing Nick to chuckle.

So far his eyes were a muddy color and would

probably go brown like his and Erica's. No doubt they would fill with tears when he took Jamie away and the baby discovered himself in strange surroundings. Better get this over quick.

Seizing the moment, he lifted the baby and propped him against his shoulder. "Come on, son. We're going to take a little ride in the car with Paul. Would you like that?"

Walter handed him the quilt and a diaper bag. His eyes sent a message to Nick that he'd better live up to his promises. "The nurse printed out Jamie's routine and the things you'll need after you get to your apartment."

"I can't thank you enough for watching over Jamie until now. I promise I'll bring him back next Saturday for a visit."

"We'll expect you." But Walter couldn't get Anne to lift her head.

"Anytime either of you wants to see him, just come by the apartment. If I'm at work, the nanny will let you in."

Anne's head flew back, revealing a face devoid of animation. "Barbara Cosgriff can't let their nanny come to you until September. There's no reason to take our grandson yet." The reproach in her voice was palpable.

"There's every reason, Anne. I miss my son and am engaging someone else until then."

"Who?" she demanded.

"I'm not sure yet. My secretary has been interviewing applicants all week. By tomorrow I expect she'll have found several for me to talk to personally. She'll do a thorough vetting. That woman is worth her weight in gold and has never let me down yet."

"What does she know about being a nanny?"

"Though I realize you can't comprehend it, she's been an exceptional working mother for me and that has never changed since she came to work eight years ago. It tells me she'll know what to look for. Keep in mind that the nanny she finds will only be with me three months until the Cosgriffs' nanny becomes free."

That was what he was saying now, yet in fact he had no idea if he would hire the Cosgriffs' nanny at all! But that revelation could keep for another day. "I plan to work shorter hours this summer, so it won't be as if Jamie's alone with her twelve hours a day."

"If you'd taken more time off to travel with Erica, you could have saved your marriage."

No. Nothing could have saved it, Anne. But to get into a postmortem with her at this stage would be futile.

"Your penthouse isn't suited to having a baby there, but somehow you insisted on Erica living there with you so you could be close to your work. She needed a real home where she could entertain."

His temper flared again, but he managed to keep it contained. "She made it into a place where she could invite her friends after the opera and the ballet. I offered to buy Sedgewick Manor in the Hamptons for her, but she preferred to stay with you because she said it suited her better. Jamie and I will manage."

Nick didn't know how yet, but he'd figure it out. He kissed the baby's silky head. "Thank the nurse for the notes. I'm sure I'll need to refer to them until I get used to the routine."

She kept her hands tightly clasped in her lap.

"The nurse said he'll be ready for another bottle when he goes down for his nap at noon."

"That's good to know. We'll be back at the apartment by then." Hopefully at that point Nick would have heard from Leah Tribe about the new nanny.

"See you next Saturday. Remember you can call anytime."

Nick turned and walked through the house with his son, still disbelieving this day had come and he was leaving the whole dreadful past behind. It was like tearing off a straitjacket.

When Paul saw him, he got out of the limo. Together they put Jamie in his new car seat. Nick could have done it without Paul's help, but he was grateful for it because it would probably have taken Nick half a dozen tries to get the confounded thing right.

The older man studied his tiny features for a minute. "I see a lot of you in him, Nick. He's a fine-looking boy."

"Blame that on his mother."

Paul patted his shoulder. "I'll drive carefully."

"I'm not worried."

He put the diaper bag on the opposite seat, then sat next to Jamie and fastened his own seat belt. As they started down the driveway, he looked around but only saw the closed front door of Hirst Hollow. It symbolized a closed life because both sets of parents had been emotionally unavailable.

You should have done this sooner, Wainwright.

But it was too late for more regrets. He needed to let the past go and concentrate on Jamie. When he looked down, he caught the baby staring at him.

Nick smiled and put out his hand so he'd grab it. His little fingers took hold with surprising strength. No tears yet. They hadn't been gone long enough for Jamie to miss the familiar faces of his nurse and grandparents.

He fought down the anger generated by his own lack of action up to now. Mired in guilt, he'd been slow to pull himself out of a depression that had its inception long before Erica's death. His estrangement from her had been one thing, but to realize his son barely knew him twisted his gut.

A chance remark by a client last week had wakened him out of his morose stupor. "With your wife gone, that new baby of yours must be a real joy to you. There's nothing like a child to make the pain go away." The comment made him realize he could be a good father.

Once his client had left the office, Nick had got on the phone to his attorney and let him know he planned to bring Jamie home where he belonged. After setting things in motion, he'd called in Leah to help him start looking for a nanny.

Nick studied the little scrap of humanity strapped in the infant seat next to him. Jamie was *his son*. Flesh of his flesh. It pained him he'd waited this long to go get him. Emotion grabbed him by the throat.

"I know this is a brand-new experience for you, sport. It is for me, too. You have no idea. I'm more the baby than you are right now and frankly, I'm terrified. You're going to help me out, aren't you?"

For answer, Jamie gave him a big yawn. A laugh

escaped Nick's throat. He'd never been responsible for anyone before. Except that wasn't exactly
true. When he'd taken on a wife, he'd promised
to love her in sickness and in health, for richer
or poorer, until death do us part.

He sucked in his breath. He'd only done the
for-richer part right. But now that he had Jamie,
he realized he'd been given a second chance and
planned to do all of it right.

Nick had come along late in life, his parents'
only child. No siblings to play with. They hadn't
allowed him a pet because both his parents didn't
want to deal with one. It was too hard, they said,
when they went on vacation.

He had two cousins, Hannah and Greg, the
children of his father's oldest brother. They rarely
played together. It wasn't until after he and Greg
were taken into the firm that he got to know him
better. In Nick's loneliness growing up, he could
see why he'd turned to books. Over time he'd
found solace in his studies and work.

Erica had been a socialite wife like her mother,
like Nick's. One eternal round of beautiful people
enjoying their financially comfortable, beautiful

lives. Not until Nick was part of the firm did his own father take an interest in him because he had a head for finances. But by then the damage had been done. They didn't have that emotional connection he'd hungered for from childhood.

He caught Jamie's busy feet with one hand and squeezed gently before letting them go again. Nick would be damned if he let the same thing happen to him and his son. Unfortunately two and a half months had already slipped by. Precious time that couldn't be recovered.

While they drove on, he opened the diaper bag and pulled out the instructions. Besides sending along some supplies, the nurse had left exact notes on her routine with Jamie, how much formula he needed, how often, nap times, that kind of thing.

He'd already arranged for the department store to deliver a crib and a new infant car seat that had come yesterday. As he thought over the list of things still to be done, his cell phone rang. Glad to see it was his secretary, he answered.

"Leah? Any success yet?"

"I've found someone I believe will suit you and the baby."

A Mary Poppins type only existed on film. "As long as she likes children and is a real motherly type and not some cardboard creation, I bow to your wisdom."

"I'll let you be the judge. She knows she hasn't been hired yet. I told her a limo would be by to pick her up at one o'clock so you could meet her and make a final decision."

"She can start today?"

"Yes. She needs a job badly."

Excellent. "What's her name?"

"Reese Chamberlain."

"Tell me more about her."

"If you don't mind, Nick, I've decided to take a leaf out of your book. You once told me you prefer to attack a new project without listening to any other voices first while you formed your own opinion. I think that's a good philosophy, especially in this case. She'll be standing in front of the Chelsea Star Hotel on West 30th."

Ms. Chamberlain really was in financial difficulty if she'd had to stay there.

"Tell Paul to look for the woman in yellow," Leah added.

"You're being very mysterious, if not cryptic. Give me something to go on."

"I'll wager she's not like anyone you ever met."

"That sounds promising."

"I hoped it would."

He made a sound in his throat. "Are you still accusing me of being a cynic?"

"I wouldn't do that. If I've made a mistake, call me later and let me know so I can keep looking for the right person."

"Do me a favor and phone Ms. Chamberlain. If she can be ready in forty-five minutes, we'll pick her up on the way to the apartment."

"She might not be available before time, but I'll see what I can do and get back to you." She clicked off.

Nick pocketed his phone, wanting to approve of Leah's assessment of the woman because there was no time to lose. Establishing a routine for the baby with the new nanny ASAP meant he'd sleep better nights. Any more weeks spent with his grandparents and Jamie would think the nurse in the starched uniform was his mother. Heaven forbid.

CHAPTER TWO

REESE had barely reached the hotel when her phone rang. She checked the caller ID and her stomach clenched. She might have known this job was too good to be true. Better to brave the bad news now and get it over with before she left for the airport. She couldn't afford to pay for another night here.

"Mrs. Tribe?"

"Ms. Chamberlain? I'm glad you answered. I've spoken with Mr. Wainwright. He's on a tight schedule and would like you to be out in front of the hotel in approximately forty minutes. Is that possible?"

She breathed a huge sigh of relief. "No problem at all."

"That's fine then. I'll let him know. Good luck to you."

"Thank you again."

After hanging up, she hurried to the dorm she'd shared with three other women. The one with Gothic piercings and purple streaks in her hair was still there stuffing everything on the bed into her backpack. She flicked Reese a glance. "How'd that interview go, honey?" Her Southern drawl was unmistakable.

"I think I got the job, but there's one more test to pass."

"I'd rather blow my brains out than be a nanny. They couldn't pay me enough."

Reese decided a response wasn't necessary. She only had a few items to pack in her suitcase and got busy.

The woman finished packing her things and turned to Reese. "It's been nice meeting you, honey. Y'all be careful now."

"You, too. Good luck finding your boy-friend."

"I'm going to need it." The door closed. Peace at last.

Reese went to the restroom to freshen up. One look in the mirror and she decided to put her hair back in a ponytail. Babies loved to tug on loose strands. Hers would be better confined. With the heat already building outside, messy limp hair and a flushed face wouldn't make the best impression. She had the kind of skin that splotched when the temperature soared.

After applying a fresh coat of lipstick, she left the bathroom, anxious to get this final interview over. With her purse and briefcase in one hand, and her suitcase in the other, she went downstairs to the lobby to check out. Unfortunately other guests anxious to get out sightseeing had the same idea. She had to wait in line.

There was a small crisis behind the desk. The computers were down. If the problem didn't get resolved fast, Reese was going to be late. Five minutes went by. She made the decision to go outside. Of course it meant losing her place in line. If her ride had come, she would ask the driver to wait while she settled her account.

Sure enough a black limo with smoked glass had pulled up in front. As she hurried toward it, a uniformed chauffeur of middle age got out. "Ms. Chamberlain?"

"Yes. I'm sorry if you've been waiting. I'm still

in line to pay my bill. Could I leave my suit-case with you? I'll run back inside. I shouldn't be much longer."

"Take your time."

"Thank you."

Ten minutes later she rushed back outside. The driver opened the rear door of the limo for her so she could get in.

"Oh—"

"Oh" was right, Nick thought to himself as the long-legged, ash-blonde female took the seat opposite him and Jamie. She brought a flowery fragrance into the limo with her. What was she? Twenty-five, twenty-six?

Her modest blouse and skirt couldn't hide the curves of a body well put together. She had to be five-eight in her bone-colored sandals and was so different from the image he had in mind of a plump, fortyish maternal type, he couldn't imagine what Leah had been thinking.

Maybe the wrong person had gotten in the limo, but she was wearing yellow.

"You're Reese Chamberlain?"

"Yes."

"I'm Nicholas Wainwright."

Her light blue eyes flared as if in surprise. "How do you do," she said in a slightly husky voice that for no particular reason appealed to him. When she saw the baby who'd fallen asleep, her eyes sparkled with life. She leaned toward Jamie, seemingly oblivious to Nick. "Oh—look how darling! All that black hair and those long, silky lashes against his cheeks."

Her gaze finally darted to Nick's. "I'm sorry to have kept you. Mrs. Tribe warned me you were a punctual man, and now I've already committed my first sin. But the computers were down at the hotel and I had to wait in line until they could check me out."

No New Yorker here or anything close. Midwest maybe? "So my driver explained. We're not in a hurry. Jamie's being very cooperative."

"He's a wonderful boy." When her eyes lifted, he could see they'd darkened with emotion. "I'm so sorry about your loss. If you decide to hire me, I promise to do everything I can to make your son as secure and happy as possible until your permanent nanny comes to live with you."

Either she was the greatest actress alive, or this was her true self. Leah was a shrewd judge of character. Something had to have appealed to his secretary for her to pick a woman whose age and looks were totally wrong for the position. She appeared too healthy to be a model, yet had the right bones and height. All Walter and Anne had to do—or anyone else for that matter—was get a glimpse of her and…

The limo was already working its way through traffic. Paul would have them deposited at the front of the apartment before long. Nick needed more information so he could decide if he would send her back to the hotel before they ever got out of the car.

"Room and board aside, what kind of salary were you expecting, Ms. Chamberlain?"

She named a figure below what he'd anticipated she would ask for. "Does that sound all right to you?"

"It's fine," he muttered, bemused by everything that came out of her mouth. "Tell me what happens when you leave me in September?"

"I'll move back to Philadelphia."

His dark brows lifted. "Another nanny position?"

She studied him with a puzzled expression. "No. I'll be in school again. I guess Mrs. Tribe failed to mention that to you."

Something had been going on with Leah he didn't understand. Without all the facts, he was at a loss. "She probably did, but I'm afraid I've been preoccupied with the arrangements for my son."

"Of course. She said your in-laws have been helping out. There's nothing like family coming to the rescue in a crisis. The baby will probably have a hard time with me at first, always looking for you or his grandparents. Were you thinking of giving me a trial run? I'll do whatever. And please don't worry. If you decide to look for someone else, I have a backup plan."

He blinked in surprise. "I thought you needed a job."

"I do, but if all else fails, I'll fly home and my

father will let me work for him this summer. It isn't what I want to do," she added, sounding far away, "but as I told you, there's nothing like family in an emergency. Dad's a sweetheart."

What had Leah said? *I'll wager she's not like anyone you ever met.*

"Where is home?"

"Lincoln, Nebraska."

So Nick was right. "What does your father do for a living?"

"He owns a lumberyard. I've helped in the office before."

"You're a long way from home. I presume college brought you to the East Coast."

"That's right. I'm a business major."

Nick's black brows furrowed. "Have you ever been a nanny?"

"No," she said forthrightly, "but I come from a large family and have done my share of tending children."

"Your mother worked, too?"

A gentle laugh escaped. "Oh, she worked— but not outside the home. Being the mother of six children is like running a major corporation.

She's been on call 24/7 since I was born." Her eyes wandered to Jamie. "There's nothing sweeter than a new baby. All they really need is lots of love between eating and sleeping."

Suddenly the door opened. Paul stood there, reminding Nick they'd arrived. He'd been so engrossed in the conversation he hadn't noticed the limo had stopped. Unless he could come up with a compelling reason not to hire her right now, taking her upstairs would be as good as a fait accompli.

While he hesitated, a piercing siren filled the air, the kind that sent an alarm through your body. It was so loud it woke Jamie, who came awake startled and crying. Before Nick could turn to get the baby's straps undone, Ms. Chamberlain had already accomplished it and plucked him out of the car seat.

In an instant she had him cuddled against her shoulder. She'd moved too fast for it to be anything more than her natural instinct to comfort. "Did that mean old siren scare you?" Her hand shaped the back of his head. "It scared me, too, but it's all right." She rocked him, giving him kisses until his frightened cries turned into whimpers.

"Sorry," she said, flicking her gaze to Nick. "I didn't mean to grab him, but that siren made *me* jump and it was easier for me to dive for him than you. His heart is pounding like a jackhammer." She started to hand the baby to Nick, but he shook his head.

"He seems perfectly happy where he is for the moment."

With those words it appeared he'd sealed his own fate. Still bemused by what had happened, he turned to an oddly silent Paul who'd already pulled the diaper bag and her suitcase out of the limo.

The baby was gorgeous. He had the overall look and coloring of his dark, striking father, but it was apparent his mother had been a beauty in her own right. No wonder Mr. Wainwright seemed to brood even as he spoke to Reese. She hadn't the slightest idea how long he and his wife had been married. What mattered was that she'd only been dead ten weeks.

Reese had undergone her own crushing pain when Jeremy had broken their engagement, but at least they hadn't been married or had a child. She didn't even want to think about the white-hot pain Jamie's father must still be in. Reese couldn't figure out how he was coping.

There was nothing she could do to alleviate his anguish. But if given the chance, she would love his little boy and make him feel secure during the hours his father was at work. By the time fall came and the new nanny took over, his daddy would have put more of his grief behind him.

Last Christmas Reese had been in agony over her split with Jeremy, but six months had gone by and she was still alive and functioning better these days. Though it would take Mr. Wainwright longer to heal, she was living proof that you didn't die of a broken heart. But he wouldn't want to hear those words right now so she wouldn't say them.

"Shall we go up?"

His deep voice broke into her reverie. She turned her head, surprised he'd already gotten out of the limo. Reese took a quick second breath because it appeared he wasn't about to send her away yet. Feeling the baby cling to her had made the whole situation real for the first time. She discovered she wanted this job very much.

"Jamie seems to have quieted down," she commented.

"Thanks to you." The comment warmed her before he reached for his son. Though he was tiny compared to his father, they looked so right together in their matching colored suits. She surmised Mr. Wainwright was in his early to mid-thirties although age was hard to tell and could add years when one was grieving.

Realizing she would become morose if she kept thinking about it, she stepped out of the limo with her purse, determined to put on a bright face for Jamie. That was her job after all. She followed his father inside a prewar brick-and-limestone building. Evidently there'd been massive renovations because the interior exuded luxury. They entered the elevator and rode to the fourteenth floor.

When the doors opened, she glimpsed a penthouse the public only got to see from inside the pages of *Architecture Digest*. The apartment itself was a piece of modern sculpture with its tall curving walls and a sweeping loft where she glimpsed a library of books and statuary. At every turn she was surprised by a bronze étagère of Mesoamerican artifacts here or a cubist painting there.

Impressions of Old World antiques, objets d'art and moiré silk period pieces flew at her like colors through a prism. There was a grand piano and a set of gorgeous Japanese screens in one section. Everywhere she looked, her gaze fastened on some treasure. A grouping of eighteenth-century furniture faced the fireplace. She wouldn't know where to begin describing the layout or furnishings of this Park Avenue address.

Months ago she'd seen an article with pictures in the *Times* of a condo something like this one that had just sold for thirty million dollars. She supposed his wealth could have come through his business endeavors.

But his breeding gave her the sense that he'd been born into the kind of family whose wealth had been one of the mainstays of Wall Street for generations. Mrs. Tribe hadn't let on. If Reese had been in her place, she wouldn't have, either.

"Since you're from Nebraska and the wide-open spaces, you'll probably find the area out here more to your liking."

She followed him across the living room's velvety Oriental rugs to the span of rounded arched windows reminiscent of the Italian masters. He opened some sliding doors. When she stepped out on the terrace, she felt as if she'd entered a park complete with trees, hedges, a pool, and tubs of flowering plants placed around with an artistic flare.

As she walked to the edge, she had an unimpeded view of Park Avenue down to the Helmsley building. The whole thing was incredible. "I would imagine after a hard day at the office, this is your favorite room, too." She saw a telescope set up at one end beyond the patio furniture. When Jamie was old enough, he'd be enthralled by everything he could see through it from this angle.

"It can be pleasant if it's not too hot. I can't say I've spent that much time out here lately, but I do use the gym every morning. It's on the upper deck of my terrace. You'll see the stairs. You're welcome to work out if you want."

"Thank you."

She sensed he was in a dark mood. Lines bracketed his mouth. "Let's go back inside. I'll let you pick the bedroom you'd like, but perhaps you'd like to freshen up first. The guest bathroom is through that door."

"Thank you. I'm pretty sure Jamie's diaper needs to be changed. Could we go to the nursery first?"

He shot her an intense glance. "For now there's only a crib in my bedroom that was delivered yesterday. I haven't decided where he should sleep yet."

So Jamie *had* been at his grandparents' from the start. Why? "I see. Well, let me wash my hands first." She slipped inside the bathroom that looked more like an arboretum with plants and flowers. After washing and drying her hands, Reese joined him just inside the sliding doors and trailed her employer through the fabulous apartment to the master bedroom with a decidedly all-male look.

It had been decorated along straight lines and contemporary furniture with accents of greens and blues. Some graphics on the walls. No frills, no sense of femininity. Above all, no family pictures. Too painful a reminder? Maybe he kept them in the living room and she hadn't noticed.

The walnut crib stood at the end of the king-size bed. It had a crib sheet but no padding. The diaper bag had been put in the room along with her suitcase. Without hesitation she reached inside the bag for a diaper. Along with a dozen of them it contained a twelve-hour supply of small, individual bottles of formula, another stretchy outfit, a shirt and a receiving blanket. She pulled it out and spread it over the top of the bed.

"If you'll lay him on this, we'll change him."

He walked over and put Jamie down. "Okay, sport. This is going to be a new experience for all of us."

Mr. Wainwright wouldn't be the first man who'd never changed a diaper. "The baby's so happy with you, why don't you undo his outfit. We'll work on this together."

Reese smiled to herself to see the good-looking, well-dressed executive bending over his son to perform something he'd never done before. He seemed more human suddenly and even more attractive.

It took him a minute to undo all the snaps and free his legs. Reese undid the tabs on the diaper. "Lift his legs." When he did, she drew the old one away and slid in the new one. "Okay. Lower him and put up the front, then fasten it with these side tabs."

The baby's body was in perpetual motion. You could hear him breathing fast with animation. "He likes all this attention, don't you." She couldn't resist kissing his tummy after his father had finished. In truth her physical awareness of Mr. Wainwright had caught her off guard.

"Great job, Daddy. You did it so fast, he didn't have a chance to get you wet." His quiet chuckle pleased and surprised her. She'd like to hear that sound more often, then chastised herself for having any thoughts of a personal nature about him.

"While you finish dressing him, I'll get rid of this." She took the soiled diaper and headed for a door she could see across the room, thinking it was the bathroom, but it led to an office where he could work at home. "Oops. Wrong room."

"The bathroom's behind me. I didn't realize it was your destination." By now he was holding Jamie against his shoulder again. They really did look gorgeous together.

Reese averted her eyes and moved past him before opening the door to the elegant bathroom. She put the diaper on the marble counter, madly compiling a mental list of all the things they would need to make his apartment baby friendly.

After washing her hands, she came out again and said, "Do you know my whole family could fit in there comfortably?" His lips twitched. When they did that, he didn't look as stressed and was too attractive by far. "How many bedrooms are there besides this one?"

"There's one across the hall from my room, and one at the other end of the apartment."

"I've been thinking… Would it be possible to move your office to that other bedroom, or to somewhere else in the apartment entirely?"

He cocked his dark head. "Anything's possible."

"It's just that your office is the perfect size for a nursery because it has a door leading into your room as well as the hall. If you put Jamie in there, he'd be close to you. I assume that's what you want. As for me, I could stay across the hall where I could hear him, too. I don't know about you, but when I was growing up, I didn't like being isolated from my parents."

He stared at her so hard, she couldn't imagine what was going through his mind, but it made her worry she might have overstepped her bounds. "What do you think?" she prodded quietly.

"It's a brilliant idea, one I would never have thought of."

"Oh, good." Reese was amazed he would admit something like that. Most men had too much pride. She liked that quality about him very much. To her alarm, she realized, there wasn't anything about this man she didn't like.

Why hadn't his wife fixed up a nursery before the baby was born? Had they lived somewhere else? Maybe he'd only recently moved in here, but why hadn't he brought everything for the baby with him?

Whatever the answer, you would have thought his wife would have taken on the job of getting prepared for a baby, but she was gone now. All he had was Reese.

"I tell you what. If you want to stay here with Jamie, maybe you could ask your driver to take me to a store where I can get all the things we need in one stop? It'll take a limo to bring back everything we require in a single trip."

When he didn't respond she said, "Or else I'll make a list for you and you buy everything while I tend the baby? Later we can move furniture and get everything set up. It's kind of fun to do together. Jamie can watch us. He's very bright and alert. By tonight we'll have this place transformed and he'll know he's home with his daddy."

She watched him reach in his pocket for his

cell phone. "I'll call Paul and tell him to meet you out in front. He'll take you to a place where I have an account. Buy whatever we need. When you get back, the concierge will arrange to get everything upstairs."

To not have to worry about money would be a first in her life. Since it was for Jamie, she would take his father at his word and enjoy her shopping spree.

"After you've returned I'll ask the chef to send up a meal for us. Are you allergic to anything?"

Chefs, a doorman, a concierge, no ceiling on expenditures— One could get used to this instantly.

"No, but thank you for asking. Are there certain foods you can't tolerate, Mr. Wainwright?"

"No."

"What about the baby?"

"So far no problems that I know of."

"Thank goodness. Excuse me for a minute while I freshen up in my bedroom."

She reached for the suitcase and briefcase and carried them across the hall to the other bedroom done in an opulent Mediterranean decor.

It had its own ornate en suite bathroom with two sinks. She would use one of them to bathe Jamie. Afterward she couldn't wait to wrap him up in the plush lavender towels hanging from a row of gilded hooks.

Reese looked around, incredulous that this was happening. Her thoughts darted to her employer. How was is it possible she'd be sleeping across the hall from the most fabulous man she'd ever met in her life?

After Ms. Chamberlain left the apartment, Nick fed the baby another bottle. He'd watched the nurse burp Jamie and had gotten that part down right. Once Jamie fell asleep, Nick laid him in the center of the bed and put the quilt over him. In the process he noticed the time on his watch. It was after three. The day had gotten away from him completely.

He reached for his cell phone and called the office. "Uncle Stan?"

"Where have you been? I need to discuss the Grayson merger with you. I've run into a snag and want your help."

"I'm aware of that, but it won't be possible today or tomorrow. Can't you talk to Uncle Phil?"

"He's at the dentist getting a new crown this afternoon."

"Then ask Greg."

"He doesn't know all the ins and outs. It's too tricky for him."

"Nevertheless I can't come in the office until Monday."

"That might be too late, Nicky." His father's younger brother had always been an alarmist.

"Sorry, but it can't be helped."

"Since when? I don't understand."

No. He wouldn't. His uncle and aunt had been childless. "Today I brought Jamie home for good."

There was a deafening silence. "I thought he—"

"He's been with his grandparents too long as it is," he broke in.

"But how will you manage?"

So far...better than Nick had thought possible. "I've hired a nanny." A totally feminine, beautiful, unexpected young woman. The image of her clutching Jamie to her while they were still in the limo—as if she was the mother—refused to leave his mind.

"I had no idea you'd even been looking for one. Your father never said a word."

"He and Mother were already in Cannes when I made the decision."

"I hear a decent one is almost impossible to come by. Is she over forty?"

His patience was running out. "Why do you ask?"

"Because anyone younger who still has their eyesight will do whatever it takes to get set up with you."

If Nick had inherited a cynical gene, it had to have come from his uncle. But in this case he wasn't worried. Leah would have done a thorough check of Ms. Chamberlain's background. He paid his secretary a salary that ensured mistakes like the one his uncle was talking about didn't happen.

"See you on Monday, Uncle Stan," Nick muttered before clicking off. Now to get busy dismantling his office. But before he did that, he changed out of his suit into something more comfortable.

To his relief, Jamie slept through the next two hours. By the time the concierge rang him at five and told him he was on his way up with Ms. Chamberlain, Nick had just wheeled the baby crib into the empty room.

He walked through the apartment to the entry and opened the door. Soon his nanny emerged from the elevator carrying bags in both hands. As she passed by him she said, "Merry Christmas." She was intriguing and amusing at the same time.

Behind her came the concierge pushing a dolly loaded with cartons. Paul brought up the rear with more bags. He winked at Nick, who was still reacting to her comment. "This bag goes in the kitchen. Then we have one more load," he whispered before heading for the other room.

"You've done the work of a thousand—" she exclaimed to Nick after the men had filed back out of the new nursery. "Jamie's going to *love* this room once we've whipped it into shape. How's he doing so far?"

She had such a vivacious personality, Nick was mesmerized. No wonder Leah had picked her. Ms. Chamberlain had to have stood out a hundred miles from any of the other nanny candidates.

"He's still asleep on my bed."

"I'll just wash my hands and peek in on him."

"While you do that I'll ask the kitchen to send up our dinner." He made the call, then started looking through the bags, curious to see what she'd purchased for one tiny baby. In a minute the concierge came through with even more cartons.

"Have fun putting all this together, Mr. Wainwright. Leave the empty boxes outside in the hall and I'll pick them up."

Nick thanked him and walked him out in time to ask the waiter to set up their dinner in the dining room. Halfway back to his bedroom he met her in the hall carrying Jamie in her arms. "This little guy was awake. I guess he could hear the noise and started to fuss. He needed a diaper change and let me handle it, but I think he wanted you to do the honors."

"Well, now that the deed is done, our food is ready in the dining room."

"That sounds good. If you'll open the carton that says *baby swing,* we can set it up in there and he can watch you while we eat. It will be perfect for him when we go out on the terrace during the day."

He hadn't seen one of those at the Hirsts'. "You want to swing?" Nick gave him a kiss on the cheek before heading into the nursery. Reese followed him and waited while he opened the carton.

"There should be some batteries taped to the inside of the lid."

"Batteries?"

"They make it swing and play music at the same time."

Though he moved millions of dollars around on paper every day, the world of a baby and all its attendant necessities had passed him by completely. Whether his boy needed a swing or not, he had one now. Thankfully it wasn't as difficult to put together as installing the base of the infant car seat in the limo. It had taken him several attempts before he'd managed to do it right.

"Let's go try this out."

"Your daddy's a genius to assemble it so fast, Jamie."

"Don't speak too soon in case it goes crashing down, taking my son with it."

"We're not worried."

He stared into her shimmering blue eyes, dumbfounded over Leah's find. "Then you should be."

CHAPTER THREE

WHEN Nick looked at her like that, Reese's heart began thudding for reasons she didn't dare explore right now.

She followed him back to the living room. The floor-to-ceiling French doors at the end had been opened to reveal a dining room that took her breath. First came the chandelier of Czechoslovakian glass. One of this kind and size was a museum piece. She thought the same thing of the massive Italian provincial hutch that lined the far wall.

Its shelving held handblown Venetian glass and stunning pieces of china no longer made. On the opposite wall was a long European hunt board with its distinctive stylized pheasants and peacocks. A still-life oil painting of fruits hung above it.

The window featured tapestries with tassels

pulled halfway down depicting various pastoral scenes. When she could tear her gaze away, it fell on the rectangular table of dark oak dominating the room. She counted sixteen chairs around. The exquisite woodwork was complemented by the upholstery fabric, a blend of rich green and cream striping on velvet.

Two candelabras with lighted tapers flanked a breathtaking centerpiece of fresh flowers including creamy lilies and roses interspersed with greenery. The top of the beautifully carved table had such a highly polished surface, everything gleamed. Two places nearest the doors had been set where their dinner awaited them.

She finally looked at her employer. "I'm afraid whoever dreamed up this masterpiece of a room didn't have that swing in mind." He'd set it on a gorgeous Persian rug at the corner of the table.

"I have to give my wife credit for much of the apartment's decor."

So they *had* lived here together. How painful this must be for him. "She had incomparable taste."

He took the baby from her and fastened him in the seat. "Let's see if he likes this." When he pressed the button, it started to swing and played "Here We Go Round the Mulberry Bush." Jamie looked at his father. The baby acted happy and it brought a ghost of a smile to his father's lips.

Mr. Wainwright's eyes unexpectedly narrowed on her features. "Your contribution to the room keeps it from feeling like a museum. Shall we eat?"

Reese could imagine the apartment felt that way to him with his other half gone out of his life. But he had his adorable son staring up at him in wonder, as if his father was the whole world to him. That had to compensate for his loss.

Leaving him to sit at the head of the table, she took her place at the side just as the song changed to another nursery rhyme. It played a medley of ten tunes.

He removed the covers from their plates, sending a mouthwatering aroma through the room. "Help yourself to coffee or tea."

"Thank you, but I'll just have water." She

poured herself a glass from the pitcher and drank a little before starting in on her food. "This roast chicken is delicious."

"I'll tell the chef. He was plucked from a five-star hotel in Paris."

"The chicken or the chef?"

His deep laugh disarmed her. "Touché."

She laughed with him. "It explains the buttery taste I love. I'm afraid I'm as bad as Julia Child. We think alike. Butter is the building block for good food."

His dark eyes flicked to hers. The candlelight reflecting in them made the irises look more brown than black. Until now she hadn't been able to decide their exact shade. "You eat a lot of it out in Nebraska, do you?"

"We Cornhuskers never heard of cholesterol," she teased, laying it on a little thick. "In truth, all of us healthy farm girls thrive on it."

One dark brow shot up. "If I offended you, I didn't mean to."

She smiled. "I know you didn't. I was just having fun."

"That's a refreshing quality of yours, Reese. Mind if I call you that?"

His genuine warmth came as a surprise. She hadn't expected a truly successful, wealthy CEO like him to be so well-rounded. It was probably that quality as much as his brilliant mind that drew people to him and made him such a paragon.

"To be honest, I hate being called Ms. Chamberlain, *Mr.* Wainwright."

He smiled. "If that was more funning on your part, I still get the hint. Call me Nick."

"Thank you. I was afraid it wouldn't happen for a while."

Another chuckle ensued. "Am I that impossible?"

Reese was already too addicted to his potent charisma. "Not at all, but I'd like Jamie to know I have a first name. Ms. Chamberlain is kind of heavy for a ten-week-old." She put her fork down. "Speaking of the baby, I know it looks like I bought out the store, but everything I purchased was for a reason. Of course I'll take anything back you don't like or find necessary."

"I'll reserve judgment until tomorrow. We've worked hard enough today and need an early night."

"The only thing we ought to do before turning in is to fix up Jamie's crib."

"What's wrong with it?"

"Nothing, but it needs a mattress cover under the fitted sheet and a bumper pad to go around the edges so he won't hurt his head against the bars. And I bought a cute little mobile with farm animals that plays tunes. Anything with bright colors and he'll reach for it."

He glanced down at Jamie. "You know what, sport? I have a feeling Reese is going to spoil you rotten."

"That's the plan," she interjected. "You can't spoil babies enough because they're too cute." She leaned over to cup his cheek.

"Would you like dessert?" he murmured.

She felt his dark gaze on her, making her so aware of him, it sent heat to her face. "I don't think I have room for any, thank you. The dinner was wonderful."

Reese started to get up from the table, ready to take the dishes into the kitchen. She assumed it lay beyond the door at the other end of the dining room. But he said, "Leave everything for the waiter. He lets himself in and out. So do the maids."

"I didn't realize." She remained in place.

"When you need a wash done for you or the baby, just put it in a laundry bag on the counter in your bathroom. You'll find them in the cupboard beneath the sinks. If you need pressing or tailoring done, phone them to indicate what you want."

She left her napkin next to her plate. "Do you always have your meals brought up?"

"No. Most of the time I eat out. Occasionally I fix something in the kitchen and sit at the island. While you're here, feel free to order whatever you want from downstairs. All you have to do is pick up the house phone and dial one for the chef's office, or two for maid service. They come in every morning. Your job is to take care of Jamie, nothing else."

"Understood."

"You're welcome to fix your own meals whether I'm home or not. Tomorrow there'll be time for you to look around the pantry and compile a list of groceries you'd like to have on hand. Dial three for the concierge. Give him the list and he'll see they're delivered."

He pushed himself away from the table and stood up to take the baby out of the swing. "Come on, Jamie. Let's see how long it takes your old man to put that mobile together."

"You've been given a reprieve on that one," Reese said, bringing up the rear. "The only thing you have to do is fasten it to the end of the crib and turn on the music. There's a small sack of batteries somewhere, but give me a minute to make up the crib first."

He moved fast on those long, powerful legs. She had to hurry to keep up with him. When they reached the nursery, she found the item for him, then quickly got busy. After she'd tied the last part of the bumper pad, she reached for Jamie.

"I'll feed him while you set up the mobile."

She darted into Nick's bedroom and got a bottle of formula out of the diaper bag, sat down on the end of his bed and fed Jamie.

"You're a hungry boy." He drank noisily. His burps were noisy, too, making her laugh. When he'd drained his bottle, she wandered back into the nursery where she found Nick watching the mobile turn while it played a song.

He glanced at her as she walked in. "I know I didn't have one of these when I was growing up."

She nuzzled Jamie's neck. "I think you're going to like what your daddy just put up." When she lowered him to the mattress, the tune drew his attention, as did the plush animals going around and around.

"Look, Nick—his cute little body is squiggling with excitement. He loves it!"

"I think you're right." When she looked up, their eyes caught and held. The intensity of his gaze made it difficult to breathe. "If you want to call it an early night, go ahead. I'll get up with him during the night. Tomorrow will be soon enough to take care of everything else and set up a schedule."

Then he looked back at Jamie with so much love, Reese was spellbound. She got the hint. He wanted time alone with his son. Nothing could be more natural or more reassuring to Jamie who, would be spending tonight in brand-new surroundings.

"I'll say good-night then and see both of you in the morning." As she reached the door, she turned around. "Thank you for giving me this opportunity. I'm very grateful. He's a precious boy."

Without waiting for a response, Reese slipped out of the nursery to the bedroom across the hall. After taking a shower and getting ready for bed, she climbed under the covers and reached for her cell phone to call her parents. It was an hour earlier in Lincoln.

"Reese? I've been hoping you'd call, honey."

"Sorry about that, Mom, but I've been so busy today, this has been my first chance to call. I've gotten myself a nanny job."

"Of course I'm happy for you, but everyone misses you."

"I miss them, but with the salary I'll be making here, I can concentrate my time on studying for the Series 7 and the Series 65. I have to take the test at the end of July before classes start again at the end of August. It shouldn't be a problem putting in the hours I need and still work around the baby's schedule." But she needed to get busy right away, which didn't give her much breathing room.

"You only have one child to look after?"

"Yes. He's ten weeks old. Oh, Mom, Jamie's the most beautiful child you ever saw." That was because his father was the most arresting male Reese had ever laid eyes on in her life. The byplay of muscles beneath his T-shirt revealed a fit masculine body. Working out in his gym on the roof every day was the reason he was so buff.

"What are his parents like? I hope they're nice. Do you think you'll all get along?"

Reese bit her lip. "There's just the father. His wife died during the birth."

"Oh, no—"

"It's very sad."

"What's his name?"

"Nick Wainwright. He's the CEO at Sherborne-Wainwright. It's the kind of brokerage company every student at Wharton would kill for in order to be able to work there. Would you believe I've been installed in his penthouse on Park Avenue? If Jackie Onassis were alive today, she would gobble it up in a second."

Her mom chuckled. "Be serious."

"I am. Who ever dreamed I'd be an honest-to-goodness nanny in a household like his?"

"How old is he?"

"It's hard to tell. Thirty-three, thirty-four maybe."

"Well…you've got a terrific head on those shoulders and broke off with Jeremy for a reason. I don't have to worry about you losing sight of your career plans just yet, do I?"

"Nothing could make me do that."

"I believe you. Destiny has already singled out my brilliant daughter for something special.

Tell me more about this financial prince of Park Avenue."

"Mom—" Reese laughed. "Financial prince... what a thing to say."

"Tell me the truth. Is he as gorgeous as Jackie's son was?"

Her mother would keel over if she ever got a look at Jamie's father. "There are no words."

"Well. Coming from you, that says it all."

Reese was afraid it did.

"Still, if I know my daughter, you won't let anything get in the way of your goal. I happen to know you're going to be a big name to contend with in the business world one day."

Reese's eyelids prickled. "Thanks for believing in me, Mom."

"Oh, I do! Just don't let those mothering instincts make you too attached to the baby. It can happen."

Reese knew it was one of the hazards of the job, but she'd deal with it. Jamie was an adorable little boy and it would be so easy to get attached to him, but Reese reminded herself that she would only be here for three months. "I love you. Give Dad and everyone else my love. I'll call you soon."

Once she'd hung up, she checked her phone messages. One was from her roommate, Pam, who'd gone home to Florida for the summer. Reese would call her sometime tomorrow.

The other call came from her study partner, Rich Bonner. He'd asked her to phone him back as soon as she could. He'd flown home to California for a break before returning to Philadelphia. Like her, he was preparing for his exams. They'd done a lot of studying together. Reese knew that Rich wanted more than just a platonic friendship with her, but she wasn't interested, not that way.

If she didn't return his call for a while, he'd hopefully get the hint. One of the problems with Rich was that he was highly competitive. As long as they remained friends, he had to be nice to her when she got higher grades than he did.

But Reese wagered that if she were ever to become his girlfriend, he'd start telling her how to live her life. Heaven forbid if she landed a better job than he did after graduation. Worse, what if she were married to him and he expected her to stay at home? Another control freak like Jeremy. Help. No more of that, please.

With a sigh, she turned off the lamp at the bedside and pulled the covers over her. Having taken Nick at his word that he would be getting up with the baby, she'd closed the bedroom door. Starting tomorrow night she'd put the new baby monitor in her room so she could hear him cry.

The day had been long and she felt physically exhausted, but exhilarated, too, because she'd found the kind of job she'd been hoping for, never dreaming it really existed. Now she didn't have to go home. Instead she could make the kind of money her father wouldn't be able to pay her by her staying right here in New York.

All she had to do was look after one little baby in surroundings only an exclusive group of people would ever know about or see. When Reese had mentioned Jackie Kennedy to her mom, she'd also been thinking of her son John Jr.'s Tribeca apartment.

It must have been over ten years ago she'd seen a few pictures of the interior following his death when she'd been a teenager. From what she remembered, it wasn't nearly on the same scale of splendor as Mr. Wainwright's fantastic residence. The architectural design for making the most of the light was nothing short of breathtaking.

Like the man himself. *Breathtaking.*

"Good morning, Reese." Nick put his newspaper down on the glass-top patio table. He'd seen her ponytail swinging as she'd stepped out on the terrace and closed the sliding door. In a modest pale orange top and jeans that still managed to cling to her womanly figure, he was going to have difficulty keeping his eyes off her.

"So *this* is where you are." She walked right over and hunkered down in front of Jamie, who was strapped in the swing wide-awake. He liked the motion, but Nick hadn't turned on the music yet. "I've been looking for you." She kissed his cheek and neck. "Hey—you're wearing a nightgown. Do you have any idea how cute you look?"

Jamie transferred his attention to her while he took little breaths as if he recognized her.

Naturally he did. Nick could have been blind-folded but would still know her by her scent. It reminded him of wildflowers. This time she kissed his son's tummy, causing him to smile. "Did you sleep through the night like a good boy?"

"He had a bottle at two-thirty and only woke up again at seven-thirty."

"Well, good for you." She tickled his chin and got him to laugh out loud. "Five hours is ter-rific. The sixty-four-thousand-dollar questions is, how's Dad?" She shot Nick a direct glance. The iridescent blue of her eyes was an extraordinary color.

"Dad's all right for an old man. What about you?"

"I got a wonderful sleep and now I'm ready to help put that nursery together."

"Not before you eat breakfast or you'll hurt Cesar's feelings."

"Chef Cesar?" she teased.

"That's right. He made a crab omelet in your honor with plenty of butter."

"Did you hear that, Jamie? I guess I'd better eat

it while it's still hot." She sat down opposite Nick and removed the cover on her plate. "Croissants, too?" Her gaze darted to the baby, who followed her movements while she ate. "We're going to have to go for a long walk in the stroller to work off the pounds I can already feel going on. But that's okay because this food is too good to resist."

Nick couldn't imagine her ever having that kind of a problem. "Coffee?"

"Please."

To his dismay he discovered Reese had another quality he liked besides her ability to have fun. She enjoyed everything and ate her meal with real pleasure. No female of his acquaintance did that, certainly not Erica, who was constantly watching her figure.

He found Reese a woman devoid of self-consciousness. For some men, it might be off-putting, but for Nick it had the opposite effect…a fact that troubled him more than a little bit. She was his nanny for heaven's sake!

After finishing her coffee, she looked across at him with a definite smile in her eyes. "Before we put our shoulders to the wheel—is there any-thing I should be worried about in the *Wall Street Journal* this morning?"

He chuckled. "Not unless you've been follow-ing news on the euro."

"Is it good or bad?"

Her question surprised him for the simple reason he couldn't imagine it being of interest to her, but she was being polite so he would return the compliment. "Overnight it staged a late surge in U.S. trading, rebounding sharply against the dollar. As a result it unwound the 'carry' trades and sent the Australian dollar and Brazilian real plunging."

Her well-shaped brows knit together. "Is that a critical situation in your eyes?"

"No, but it has some global economists rattled."

"Well, if you're not upset, then I'm certainly not going to be." She got to her feet. "If you don't mind, I'll carry him back to my bedroom and give him a quick bath. Then we're all yours."

Nick had no idea what to make of her. But as he watched her disappear with Jamie, he decided it didn't matter because his son appeared to be in the best of hands. Yesterday morning he couldn't have foreseen the changes that had already taken place since he'd picked her up in front of the hotel.

He gathered up the swing and headed for the nursery. After putting it in the corner, some impulse had him walking across the hall to her room. She'd left all the doors open, so he continued on through. When he reached the bathroom, the sight that greeted him brought a lump to his throat.

Reese had filled one of the sinks with water. While she cradled the back of Jamie's head in the water, she washed his scalp and talked to him in soothing tones. His son was mesmerized. Slowly she rinsed off the baby shampoo, then took a bar of baby soap and washed his limbs. With the greatest tenderness she turned him over and washed his back. He made little cooing sounds Nick felt resonate in his body.

Without conscious thought he reached for one of the towels and held it up for her. Their eyes met for an instant. She said, "While you dry him off, I'll find him a new outfit to put on."

Nick cuddled his boy to him, uncaring that he was still wet. He smelled so sweet. As he felt Jamie burrow into his neck, a feeling of love flowed through him so intense, he was staggered by it.

"What do you think?" she asked when he appeared in the doorway to the nursery, holding up three outfits. "The white with the tiger, the green with the fish or the navy with the Snoopy?"

"Maybe we should let Jamie decide." He turned him around in his arms and walked over to her. "I wonder which one he'll go for."

She laughed in anticipation, watching him closely. "His eyes keep looking at the dog."

"Every boy should have one," Nick declared. "Snoopy it is."

"Did you have a dog?"

"No. What about you?"

"We went through three before I left home."

Reese had the diaper ready. Nick lowered his son in the crib and put it on with no hesitation this time. She handed him the one-piece fitted suit with no legs. After he'd snapped it, he picked him up again.

"Let me brush his hair and then he's ready for the day." As she lifted her arm, it brushed against Nick's. An unconscious thing to be sure, the lightest of touches. But he'd felt her warmth against his skin and the next thing he knew it had swamped his sensitized body.

He hadn't been intimate with a woman since the last time he'd slept with Erica. That was the reason for this total physical reaction. *It had to be*.

"First things first," she declared. "There's a diaper pail around here somewhere with a scented deodorizer. Ah—" She opened one of the cartons. "Just what we need." After lining it, in went the diaper. Then she lifted her head, causing her ponytail to swish like quicksilver. "Where do you want the crib to go?"

He struggled to concentrate. "How about the far wall. The sun won't reach him there when the shutters are open, and it will leave both doorways free."

"Perfect." She moved things out of the way so

she could roll it into position across the hard-wood floor.

Nick settled Jamie back in his swing and they got to work opening all the boxes. While he put the stroller together, she stacked diapers, baby wipes, powder, baby cream, lotion and ear swabs in the changing-table compartments. After watching her bathe the baby with nonallergenic products, he realized there was a reason for everything she'd bought.

"I'm glad you took the Oriental rug away. I can't wait for you to see the baby furniture," she said as he reached for one of the bigger cartons.

Curious himself, Nick opened the box and discovered a child's antique white dresser with olive-green trim and a Winnie the Pooh hand-painted over the drawers. The next box held a child's chair in the shape of Piglet. A big Eyeore dominated the oval hook rug. In another carton he found a lamp whose base was shaped like a honey pot. The last carton was the biggest. When he opened it, he found an adult rocking chair with Owl as the motif.

"That's so you can sit in here and feed him

while you rock him to sleep." She'd thought of everything. The set charmed him. *She* charmed him.

He took all the boxes out of the apartment and piled them in the hall. When he came back, Reese had placed the furniture around and had put a soft, furry Winnie the Pooh in one corner of his crib.

"You've turned this room into the Hundred Acre Wood. I like it."

She whirled around with an anxious look on her face. "Honestly?"

"I doubt there's another nursery more inviting. Jamie will grow up loving to be in here. Thank you for helping me." She was an amazing person who had the knack of making everything exciting.

"I haven't had so much fun in years."

Neither had he. The ramifications of that admission were beginning to haunt him. "It's noon. We need a break."

Reese nodded. "I think your son is ready for another bottle." She finished putting the outfits she'd bought into the dresser drawers.

"As soon as I wash my hands, I'll be right back to try out the rocker with him."

When Nick returned a few minutes later he found her putting more things on top of the dresser. Besides a large, colorfully illustrated edition of Winnie the Pooh, plus a leather-bound book that said *Baby's Memories,* she'd added a pacifier, a couple of rattles, some infant pain-killer, a baby thermometer, his little brush and a box of tissues.

In an incredibly short period of time she'd written Jamie's signature on the face of his apartment. Now it was *their* home, father and son.

At the thought of what would have happened if he hadn't hired her, he experienced real terror because it had opened up an old window of time. For a moment he'd glimpsed the painful gray emptiness of yesterday. He wanted that window closed forever so he wouldn't have to know those emotions again.

Needing to feel his son's wiggly body, he drew him out of the swing and they sat down in the rocker. Reese had put the bottle of formula next to it. While Nick fed him, she placed a burp cloth over his shoulder. He felt her gaze and could tell something was on that fascinating mind of hers. "I'll be right back."

Before long she returned with her phone and started snapping pictures of him and Jamie, of the room itself. "I'll get these photos made into prints and start his scrapbook. My mom kept one for each of us and I still look at mine. When you get time, give me any photos you'd like to add."

"I'll do that." When he'd separated from Erica, he'd instructed the maids to put the wedding album and photos in the dresser drawer of the bedroom at the other end of the hall.

"While you're at it, if you have his birth certificate and the picture they took of him at the hospital, I could add it," Reese suggested. "There's a family tree in his book where I can put in pictures of you and his mother, and his grandparents. After he's older, he'll pore over them for hours."

Nick smiled as the ideas rolled from her. She seemed to really care about Jamie and his future. She was remarkable.

"Later on I'll see what I can dig up."

"Good." She took one more picture of the stuffed animal in the bed. "We'll call his baby book *The Penthouse at Pooh Corner.*"

Nick broke into laughter. He couldn't help it, even though it startled Jamie, who fussed for a minute before settling down again. Her way of putting things was a never-ending source of delight.

In the doorway to the hall she said, "You two deserve some quality time together so I'm going to leave you alone. While you're feeding him, would you mind if I took a tour of your apartment?"

"This is your home for the next three months. I want you to treat it as such."

"Thank you."

Actually Reese's request was an excuse to go back to her room. She'd have all summer to admire the treasures in Nick's home and much preferred to do it when she had the apartment to herself.

The important thing here was to give him time

alone with Jamie. Tomorrow he'd have to go back to work. Today was a gift he could enjoy with that adorable little boy who was an absolute dream to take care of.

For the moment she needed to acquaint herself with his kitchen. The disposable bottles of formula the nurse had sent in the diaper bag would be gone in another couple of feedings. Reese had bought the same brand of powdered formula and a set of bottles yesterday. She needed to run them through the dishwasher.

When she reached the fantasy kitchen, she wished Julia Child had been with her so she could hear her go into ecstasy. Now *there* was a chopping block befitting a piece of veal she could slap down and pound the life out of before she turned it into mouthwatering *escalope de veau*.

While Reese was still in a bemused state, the house phone rang. It sounded so loud, she jumped in surprise and hurried to pick it up for fear it would wake Jamie, who was probably asleep by now.

"Hello?"

"Ms. Chamberlain? This is Albert, the concierge."

"Oh, yes. Thank you for your help yesterday, Albert."

"That was quite a collection of things you bought. How's the nursery coming along?"

"We've got it all put together."

"That sounds like Mr. Wainwright. Does the work of ten without thinking about it. I'm calling because his in-laws have arrived and want to come up. Is he available to talk to?"

Reese was pretty sure Nick wasn't expecting anyone, but that wasn't for her to decide. "Just a moment and I'll tell him to pick up the phone." She put the receiver down and hurried through the apartment to the nursery.

The baby had finished his bottle and lay against Nick's shoulder with his little eyelids fluttering. Reese hated to disturb them, but she had no choice. She walked around in front of him. He raised those dark eyes to her face in question.

"Albert is on the phone. He says your in-laws are downstairs and want to come up," she mouthed the words.

Nick brushed his lips against the baby's head before getting to his feet in one lithe male move. "I'll talk to him from the phone in my bedroom."

After he left with Jamie, she walked back to the kitchen. The second she heard Nick's deep voice, she hung up the phone.

The bottles were still waiting. She removed the packaging before loading them in the dishwasher. The lids and nipples fit inside the little basket.

Beneath the kitchen sink she found a box of dishwasher detergent that hadn't been used yet. She undid the seal and poured some in the dispenser. Pretty soon she had the machine going on the wash/dry cycle.

While she waited, she opened the canister of powdered formula and read the directions. Once the items were dry and sterilized, she measured enough instant formula into each, before adding the required amount of water.

Nick chose that moment to bring an attractive, well-dressed older couple into the kitchen. "Sorry. I was just making up Jamie's formula." She wiped her hands with a clean cloth.

Nick's eyes glimmered with some emotion she couldn't put a name to. "No problem. Reese Chamberlain? I'd like you to meet Jamie's grand-parents, Anne and Walter Hirst. They wanted to be introduced."

"Of course." She walked over to shake their hands. "It's a pleasure to meet you."

CHAPTER FOUR

REESE had once seen the original oil painting of Grant Wood's *American Gothic* in Chicago. It depicted a farmer and a woman with stern faces standing in front of a white farmhouse. In the man's hand was an upturned pitchfork.

Though Nick's in-laws were good-looking people, they could have been the models for the painting. Mr. Hirst wore an expression of dislike in his eyes as he said hello. She could imagine him coming to life to poke her with his farm implement. His wife remained stiff and mute. Reese felt for the brunette woman who'd lost her daughter so recently. Lines of grief were still visible on both their faces. Pain, pain, pain.

This had to be brutal on Nick, who was still trying to deal with the loss of his wife, too. He shifted Jamie to his other shoulder. Looking at Reese he said, "I explained that the three of us are still getting acquainted. Leave what you're doing and come with us while I show them the nursery."

There was enough authority underlining his words for Reese to know he expected her to join them. Why, she didn't know, but she did his bidding without question. When they reached the nursery she heard a sudden gasp from Jamie's grandmother.

"What a surprise!" his grandfather said. "Where did your office go?"

"It's dismantled in another bedroom. As you can see, we're coming along thanks to Ms. Chamberlain, so you don't need to be concerned about the baby's welfare. Sit down in the rocking chair and hold Jamie. He just had his bath and a bottle. I doubt he'll be hungry for another couple of hours."

Nick handed her the baby. Reese held her breath, hoping he wouldn't start to cry having to leave Nick's arms. To her relief he just looked up quietly at his grandmother. It was a sweet moment. Jamie had a wonderful nature.

"I'll get a chair from my room for you, Walter."

Nick was back in a second. "Now you can enjoy him together." With wooden movements, he sat down next to his wife.

By tacit agreement Reese left the nursery with Nick and they headed for the kitchen. "What can I do to help?"

Aware of his body close to hers, she was all thumbs. "I just need to finish off making up these bottles." Nick found the lids and tops and before long the task was done and eight fresh bottles had been put in the fridge.

"I had a feeling they'd make a surprise visit," he murmured, "but not before tomorrow."

What he meant was, he knew they'd show up when Reese was alone to see how she was handling their grandson. But by their appearance today, it was clear they hadn't been able to wait that long.

"They're missing Jamie," she said. "Who wouldn't? He's as good as gold. Not one tear yet."

Nick nodded. "I know. I've been waiting."

"Not all babies have his wonderful disposition. It should ease your mother-in-law's mind that he's adapting so well to the change in surroundings."

He trapped her gaze. "That's because you haven't given him a chance to get upset. When I put in for a nanny, I never thought Mary Poppins would actually pop inside the limo."

Reese's mouth curved upward. His comment took the chill off the remembered moment when his in-laws had first looked at her as if she was an alien. "I'm afraid there's only one of those."

Better that Nick saw Reese as a fictional character.

Unfortunately she couldn't say the same thing about him. Meeting him had caused her to view him as someone very real and charismatic in spite of his deep sorrow, or maybe even because of it. Not for a second could she afford to forget this was a man who'd just lost his wife. It hadn't even been three months. Reese needed to focus on Jamie and nothing else.

"To be honest, I was afraid I'd pop in that limo and find Captain Von Trapp surrounded by seven precocious children all needing individual attention at the same time."

His low laughter rang in the spacious confines of the modern kitchen. No matter how hard she fought against it, the pleasing masculine sound connected to every atom in her body. She caught Nick's gaze and something intense passed between them, stealing Reese's breath.

"Nick?" Both of them turned in the direction of his mother-in-law's voice. The interruption had spoiled a conversation she'd been enjoying, and something else had passed between them, too, that Reese wasn't prepared to think about just yet. "We'd like to talk to you for a minute please."

Her brittle words expressed in that demanding tone meant she'd heard them laughing together. Reese feared it had been like an affront to her sensibilities. This was awful. Nick shouldn't have come into the kitchen with her.

"Of course, Anne." He glanced back at Reese. "Excuse me. Why don't you call down and order sandwiches and salad for us. Have them set up our lunch on the terrace. Cesar knows what I like."

"All right." Reaching for the phone, she gave Nick's order to the kitchen and asked them to add a pot of coffee. The waiter was to bring their lunch up to the patio table.

Relieved to be alone at last, Reese tidied away the things she'd used in the kitchen until it was once again spotless, then she walked out to the terrace, the only safe place in the apartment at the moment. While she waited for the food to come, she looked through the telescope. Once she'd made some adjustments, she had a bird's-eye view of one part of the Big Apple. Starting tomorrow she'd take Jamie out exploring in the stroller. Central Park was only two blocks away.

Last year she and Pam had come to New York for a few days on the train, but they'd been short on time and money. They'd ended up seeing one Broadway show and spent two days visiting the Metropolitan Museum of Art. That was it. The equivalent of a grain of sand in the middle of the Sahara.

"Ms. Chamberlain?" She lifted her head from the eyepiece and discovered a uniformed waiter with dark hair transferring plates from a cart to the table. His black eyes played over her with obvious male interest. He was probably in his early twenties. "I know I haven't seen you before. I'm Toni."

"Hello."

"I understand you're the new nanny."

"That's right."

"I work here Thursdays through the weekend."

"Do you like it?"

He grinned. "I do now. If you want anything, call down to the kitchen when I'm on duty and ask for me."

"I believe we have everything we need," a deep, masculine voice answered for her. Nick had come out on the terrace, surprising both of them. He had an aura that could be intimidating. Just now he sounded vaguely dismissive.

"Good afternoon, Mr. Wainwright." Toni took hold of the cart and left the terrace without delay.

"Was he bothering you, Reese?"

She shook her head. "He was being friendly. That's all." She walked over to the table with its large white umbrella and sat down beneath it. "Are your in-laws still here?"

He took a seat opposite her. "No. After Jamie went to sleep, they left to meet friends for lunch. Otherwise I would have invited them to have a meal with us."

"Do you think this visit has helped them?"

Nick took the covers off their dishes. She hadn't had a club sandwich in years. "I'm sure it didn't, but there wasn't anything they could voice a complaint about. It's apparent that with you here, everything's under control."

But Reese knew they *had* made scathing remarks about her. If the looks Mrs. Hirst had given Reese in the kitchen could inflict damage, she would have been vaporized in an instant.

"Earlier Walter told me Anne was…fragile," Nick added, as if he were choosing his words carefully. "After the way they both behaved today, I can see they're still not happy with the idea of my bringing Jamie home. I should have made the break sooner."

Reese sensed he was in a brooding mood. "It's hard to make decisions when you're grieving."

"You have some knowledge of it?" He'd posed the mild question while devouring his sandwich.

"My fiancé and I broke up at Christmas. It hit me very hard, but I couldn't compare it to your loss. When you have a child born into the world, you don't expect to have to carry on without your wife."

A bleak look entered his eyes. "Erica was in good health until she went into the hospital. Her labor wasn't normal. By the time she got there, the placenta had torn and she'd lost too much blood faster than they could replenish it. The doctor performed a Cesarian before Jamie got into trouble."

"Thank heaven for that," she whispered. "He's a little angel."

He studied her through a veiled gaze. "Does that mean you're not ready to back out of our contract yet?"

"If you knew me better, you'd realize I'd never do that, but I'm assuming your in-laws don't have much faith in me. From their perspective I suppose it's understandable."

"I'm very pleased you're here to help with Jamie, so let's not worry about them. As you said, when a person is in mourning, their emotions are in turmoil. Nothing would help them but to have Erica back."

Nick was talking about himself, too, obviously. Reese didn't know how he was functioning. The best thing to do was change the subject.

"I've been thinking. How do you feel about my taking Jamie out and about in the stroller tomorrow? Just short little forays at first. Depending on how he does, maybe longer ones."

"That's fine. Later today we'll program your cell phone so you can call me or Paul at any time. When you want to take Jamie farther afield, arrange it with him. He'll drive you to spots where you can explore to your heart's content. I'll give you a remote to the penthouse to keep all the time. All I ask is that you check in with Albert coming and going. It's for your safety."

In other words, with Nick's kind of money he would be a natural target if someone decided to arrange a kidnapping. Only now was she beginning to realize what an enormous responsibility she'd taken on. "I'll be extremely careful with him, Nick."

"I have no doubt of it." He finished his salad. "I'll open a bank account for you first thing in the morning so you'll have funds to draw on."

"Thank you."

"We haven't discussed your hours yet. If I can depend on you Monday through Friday until five every day, then you can be free to do as you wish the rest of the time. How does that sound?"

Incredibly generous. "I couldn't ask for a more perfect arrangement. But please feel free to depend on me if something comes up in the evening or on a weekend and you need my help."

"If that should happen, I'll pay you overtime."

"That won't be necessary. Being allowed to live here in such luxury with all my meals paid for is like another salary in itself. I wouldn't dream of taking more money than we agreed on." She helped herself to the salad.

An amused gleam entered those dark eyes. To her chagrin her pulse sped up. The phenomenon kept happening the more she was around him.

"Since we have that settled, are there any questions you want to ask me?"

"There's only one I can think of right now. Do you know when Jamie's supposed to go in for his next checkup?"

"The nurse indicated he saw the doctor three weeks ago. I'm going to be taking him to a new pediatrician here in the city named Dr. Wells. I'll give him a ring tomorrow and find out when he wants to see him. They'll send for his records right away."

"I think that's wise in case he needs another immunization soon."

He sat back in the chair to drink his coffee. One of the first things she'd noticed in the limo yesterday was that he didn't wear a wedding ring. In one way she thought it odd because his wife's death had been so recent. On the other hand, maybe he'd never worn one, or possibly he didn't like rings of any kind. *And maybe you're thinking about him way too much for your own good.*

"If there's anything you want to do for the rest of the afternoon, take advantage of the time,

Reese. I plan to get a little work done around here and do a few laps in the pool."

"How can you do any work when your office is in shambles?"

A chuckle escaped his throat. "I'll worry about it later."

"The mess will still be there later. Why don't we tackle the other bedroom while Jamie's out for the count? I'll feel much better if we set it up for you. Don't forget I'm the one who managed to get everything knocked out of whack. Kind of like the little kid who comes along and destroys the puzzle you just put together."

His haunting smile turned her heart over. "Okay, let's get busy." He rose to his tall, imposing height. "But when we're through, I'll take care of Jamie until I leave for work in the morning."

"He'll be thrilled with all your attention."

Hurrying ahead of him, she walked through the apartment to peek on the baby, who was fast asleep. He looked so precious with his arms and legs spread out, his little hands formed into fists.

"Not a care in the world," Nick murmured near her ear, surprising her. She could feel the warmth from his hard body. For a moment she had the urge to lean into him and cling. Almost dizzy from unbidden longings, she turned away. But in the next instant she spied a glint of pain in those dark orbs and despised herself for being so aware of him when his thoughts had absolutely nothing to do with her.

Leaving them alone, she rushed out of the nursery and down the hall to the other bedroom. The room was a vision of white and café-au-lait with an exquisite white lace throw over the down-filled duvet.

White lace curtains hung at the huge window that gave out on a fabulous view of the city. There was a love seat with a jacquard design in the same colors and a white rug with a deep pile in a geometric design of coffee and beige.

When Nick came in she said, "This is a beautiful room. Luckily it's big enough to accommodate everything if we move the love seat against that other wall. What would you think if we put your desk in front of the window where you can look out? If it gets too bright you can always draw the sheers.

"And on the left here we'll set up your computer system. Keep in mind that if you get tired, you only have to take a few steps to the bed."

His hands went to his hips in a purely male stance. He glanced around at all his state-of-the-art equipment without saying anything. She wandered over to the window and looked out while she waited for him to make a decision.

"I've got a better idea." Reese turned to him, curious to hear what he had to say. She felt his penetrating glance. "I'm going to give up having an office altogether and work from a laptop in my bedroom when I'm forced to."

"I don't understand." She was incredulous.

"There are only so many hours in the day. If I can't accomplish what I need to do at the office, then I'll turn it over to someone else. I have my son to think about now." His explanation sounded more like a declaration, as if his mind had been somewhere else. "Please feel free to enjoy the rest of your day. I'm going out to the pool."

Reese had been dismissed. Now that their

business was concluded, naturally he had other plans that didn't include her. Silly how bereft she felt.

Needing to shake the feeling, Reese went to her bedroom to start studying. But an hour later she realized she'd been going over the same section of work a dozen times and nothing was sinking in. All she could think of was a pair of dark eyes that set her heart rate fluttering.

What she needed was a good walk in the park to clear her head.

"Albert?" Nick approached the front desk at three in the afternoon. "Has Ms. Chamberlain gone out with Jamie yet?" It was Friday. He'd turned over some work for one of the office staffers to finish up so he could come home early and spend it with Jamie.

"She left maybe a half hour ago."

"Thank you."

Disappointment crept through him because it wasn't only his son he'd been longing to see. All week he'd found himself watching the clock. When it was a quarter to five, he'd called Paul to be out in front of the building to drive him home. Today he couldn't take it any longer and knew he had raised eyebrows when he'd taken off from work two hours before time.

He realized that their constant togetherness over those first two days had spoiled him. Now, Nick missed talking to Reese. She was the most alive woman he'd ever met. Intelligent. Her conversation stimulated him and there was no question Jamie adored her.

Since he had no legitimate reason to prevent her from doing what she wanted with her spare time, he usually took his son up on the roof to the gym and worked out in front of him.

Throughout the week she hadn't called down to the kitchen for dinner once. That gave him no opening to join her. Apparently she liked fixing her own food and ate before he arrived, frustrating him no end.

Not able to take it any longer, he broke his own rule and phoned her. She answered on the fourth ring. "Hello, Nick? Are you phoning from your office?"

Her voice sounded tentative, if not a trifle

anxious. He brushed aside the thought that he knew her voice so well already, knew how she was feeling simply from the tone of it. He had to remind himself that as much as he enjoyed Reese's company, she was only temporary in his and Jamie's life.

"No. Where are you and Jamie?"

"At the park. Is anything wrong?"

He sucked in his breath because it seemed there had to be some kind of emergency in order for him to be with her at a different time than the schedule dictated. The schedule *you* established, Wainwright!

"I was able to tie up work early and decided to spend the rest of the day with my son."

"I'll come right home then."

"That won't be necessary. Tell me where to find you."

Nick heard her hesitation. He didn't know if it was because she wasn't sure of her exact location, or if she didn't want his company. If it was the latter, was it because she was afraid to be alone with him? In his gut he knew she wasn't indifferent to him, but maybe she didn't want the relationship between them to move to a more personal level. He knew it would be a mistake to blur the lines between them, but Nick was becoming more and more enchanted with Reese.

He grimaced when he thought she might be in contact with her ex-fiancé. Was it possible she still had feelings for him? Nick had too many questions for which there were no answers yet.

"We're in front of the Sweet Café watching the sailboats."

"Don't leave. I'll see you shortly."

Once he'd hung up, he shrugged out of his suit and changed into more casual clothes. To save time, he had Paul drop him off near the east rim of the pond.

A mild breeze kept the sun from being too hot. Tourists and locals came here in any kind of weather, but there were more people than usual milling about this afternoon. Quite a few of them were pushing children in prams and strollers. Nick scanned the area looking for Reese's ponytail. She didn't appear to be around.

One knockout blonde with hair attractively tangled caught his eye over by the water where she was examining one of the sailboats. She wore a filmy layered top in blues and greens over a pair of jeans defining womanly hips. Her slender yet rounded body reminded him of someone. He moved closer and suddenly his heart pounded with ferocity because he saw Jamie in the stroller in front of her.

"Reese?"

She whipped around, causing her wavy ash-blond hair to swish against the top of her shoulders. The change of hairstyle had thrown him. He couldn't decide which one he liked better. Her hair had the kind of texture he'd love to work his fingers into.

At first glance her eyes flickered, causing them to reflect the blue off the water. They seemed to search his for a long moment before she averted them and leaned over to pull Jamie out of his seat.

"Look who's here." The second Jamie saw Nick, he grew more animated and squirmed to reach him. "You know your daddy all right." Reese gave a gentle laugh as she handed him over.

Nick kissed his son, rocking him for a minute

while he enjoyed the smell of her flowery scent on the baby's cheeks and neck. "Have you missed me today? I know I've missed you." He pressed a kiss to Jamie's tummy, provoking more smiles and laughter.

Today she'd put him in the green suit with the grouper fish on the front. In his tiny white socks and white high-tops, the picture he made tugged at Nick's heart. He was proud to claim him and grateful for the meticulous care Reese took of him.

He flicked his gaze to her. "Have you walked to the north end to see the Alice in Wonderland statue?"

She nodded. "It's wonderful. I particularly loved the Mad Hatter. I can't wait until Jamie's old enough t—" She stopped midsentence. He found it fascinating how an unexpected flush spilled into her cheeks.

"To *what*?" he prodded, already knowing the answer.

"I have a tendency to run on sometimes. Obviously I won't be around when he's older… it's just sometimes difficult to think about not seeing this little one grow up." Nick was gratified to find her this attached to Jamie already. In truth, for the past week he'd been imagining a future that included the three of them. Since the moment he'd brought her to the penthouse, he'd been happier than he'd ever been in his life.

He couldn't pin it down to any one thing or moment. All he knew was that she was on his mind to the point it was interfering with his concentration at the office. "Let's grab a bite while we're here. Have you eaten?"

"I hadn't planned to until we got back to the penthouse."

"Are you hungry?"

"I have to admit a salad and lemonade would hit the spot." No doubt she kept her expenses down by not spending money on food.

"I'm hungrier than that." Since the advent of Reese in his life, his appetite had grown. Food tasted better. The sky looked bluer. When he woke up in the morning, the world seemed filled with new possibilities. He looked down at his son. "What about you, sport?"

Reese answered for him. "I'm sure he wouldn't turn down a bottle. It's warm out here."

With Jamie against his shoulder, Nick pushed the stroller. Together they made their way to an empty table and sat down beneath the umbrella, welcoming the shade. As he looked around, it dawned on him he hadn't been here in years. He'd been so busy making money for the brokerage, this part of life had passed him by completely.

"Here's a bottle for him." Reese handed him a burp cloth, too.

"Thank you." His breath caught when their eyes met. "The waiter's coming over. Will you order me a steak sandwich and coffee while I feed Jamie?"

The baby nestled in his arm, eager for his formula. He was hungry and virtually inhaled it, then let out several burps loud enough to bring some other diners' heads around with a smile.

Laughter bubbled out of Reese. He loved hearing it. "Your son would be welcome in some parts of the world where it's polite to burp after a good meal."

He continued to rub Jamie's back in order to

get out all the air. By the time his eyes fluttered closed, their food had arrived. Nick lowered him into the stroller and put the canopy down to shield him from the sun.

While Reese ate her salad, he attacked his sandwich. "Did I tell you I'm taking him to his grandparents in the morning?"

She nodded. "I bet they can't wait to see him."

"Next time I'll take you with us."

A shadow crossed over her lovely face. "Why would you do that?"

"For one reason, you'll be ready for a change of scenery. For another, Jamie is already attached to you. Another week of enjoying your exclusive attention and he'll have a hard time being separated for a whole day. With you along to reassure him, things will go better." He could tell by the shadows in her eyes she was worried about it.

"Don't be concerned. You'll be free to walk around certain parts of the grounds. Hirst Hollow is open to the public on Saturdays. You'll be enchanted with the flower gardens."

Reese finished her lemonade. He could

practically see her mind taking it all in, working up a protest. After she put her glass down, she didn't disappoint him. "No matter what, your mother-in-law won't be enchanted to see the nanny along for the ride, especially this nanny!"

"Anne's going to have to get used to it. You're an integral part of my household."

"But Jamie doesn't come from a normal household."

"Go on," Nick urged, drinking the rest of his coffee. He was curious to hear the words she was getting ready to spout from lips he suddenly realized he'd love to taste.

"You don't really want me to spell it out."

"You're wrong," he fired back. "I'm fascinated by everything you have to say on the subject."

"If I told you, it could be taken as an insult, and that's the last thing I would want to do when I've been given a dream job."

"At least do me the courtesy of telling me how my son's home is *not* normal. I have to work, and I need someone to look after Jamie—what's wrong with that?"

He was prepared to hear that he made the kind of money that separated him from the masses, but she said something else instead—something that touched on that painful area of his soul no one else knew about or understood.

"In the short time I've worked for you, I've learned that Jamie is a Hirst and a Wainwright, two blue-blooded American families."

"You mean we only breathe the rarified atmosphere of the elite upper class from England going back several hundred years? You're right, Ms. Chamberlain. Someone put it much better than I could. 'In our world men were better than women, horses better than dogs, and Harvard better than anything.'"

Her cheeks turned to flame, but she held his gaze. "I should never have brought this up."

"Why not? It's the truth. Did you know the Wainwrights have had horses on Long Island going back at least two hundred years? Nothing's more important than pedigree and belonging to the right clubs. Not even marriages have as much significance as long as the principles belong to that exclusive world where the women provide the decoration.

"Everyone has rank, some higher than others. One is aware of his social placement at all times. That's only the outer shell we're talking about. Unlike the soft meat of the crab, their inner stuffing is even harder. It blinds them to the loving and understanding of their own children."

As he spoke, emotion darkened her eyes.

"Erica's and my family share an ancestry that has been in love with itself for generations. They've continued to hone the 'right' way to do things to a fine art while at the same time distancing their offspring by their criticism and lack of affection."

He heard Reese's sharp intake of breath before she said, "For that very reason certain things aren't done, like hiring an unsuitable nanny, someone like me."

"Correct. The way you hug and kiss Jamie all the time, you're probably the most unsuitable nanny in existence, which makes you perfect for the job."

Her delicately arched brows knit together. "That sounded like a declaration of war."

"War…divorce… Ultimately they're the same thing. It's time the cycle of neglect ended, starting with Jamie."

"So you're using me for a guinea pig?"

Nick nodded without shame.

"Mrs. Tribe mentioned that you'd be hiring another nanny in the fall. What about her?"

"Since my mother-in-law was the one who arranged for her in the first place, I'll let her fix the mistake. Barbara Cosgriff's another blue blood. She and Anne make up part of a very elite circle. The Cosgriffs won't be in need of their nanny by September, therefore, they're delighted to do this favor for my mother-in-law, who spoke for me without my permission, something she's good at doing."

"So whom do you plan to hire?"

"I'm not sure of anything yet, but it goes without saying that whoever she is, she'll be entirely unsuitable."

A small sad smile broke the corner of Reese's

wide mouth. "You're a clever man gaining my sympathy so I'll be a willing accomplice."

"Let's just say that for Jamie's sake, I'd like your help. Are you with me on this?"

Her gaze darted to the baby, who was just starting to wake up. She let out a troubled sigh. "You're my employer. I need this job and I love Jamie, so I'll do my best for you."

Nick ignored the little dart he felt when she referred to him as her employer. He hoped she might be inclined to do it for him. Shaking this off, he pulled out his wallet and put some bills on the table. "You have another full week before I force you to face the dragon. Put the thought away until you have to deal with her."

"That's not so easy to do."

"But possible. Remember I've had longer practice at this than you." He stood up. "If you'll push the stroller, I'll carry Jamie back to the car. He loves his bath so much, I think I'll take him for a little swim and see how he does. Have you been swimming yet?"

She hurried to keep up with him. "I don't have a suit."

"But you *can* swim?"

"Yes."

"In my teens I did a lot of sailing. It's a sport I'd like to do with my son. If he's going to share that love with me, then he needs to start getting used to the water. Already he feels safe with you. The next time you go out with Jamie, buy yourself one. Consider it your uniform and put it on my account."

If she wanted to squirm her way out of that, *too bad*.

CHAPTER FIVE

ON SATURDAY, Reese tried to study, but finally gave up. With Nick and Jamie gone from the penthouse, she was at a totally loose end. After fixing herself a sandwich for lunch, she took off for Macy's at Herald Square.

The crowded ten-story department store contained everything including the unimaginable. One would have to be here days to see it all. She ended up spending hours walking around. Eventually she found some swimsuits on sale for her and Jamie.

With Father's Day coming up, she shipped her dad a small framed picture of New York showing Park Avenue. She slipped in a note telling him to hang it in his office.

While she was looking at the toys, she discovered a wooden hand-painted toy sailboat in sky-blue with a white canvas sail Jamie could give his father. It was the perfect size to fit on a desk or a dresser. The artist on hand personalized it on the keel for her with quick-drying black paint. *The Flying NJ.* When it was finished, she asked the salesgirl to gift wrap it.

Since she was in the right place, she purchased some doughnut toys and a colorful octopus that played classical music when you touched the tentacles. By the time she got back to the apartment, it was after seven.

As she turned down the hall to her bedroom, she almost bumped into Nick. "Oh—I didn't realize you were home." Her pulse raced out of control to see him standing there in tan trousers and a midnight-blue silk shirt. He looked and smelled marvelous.

His dark eyes took swift inventory of her in her jeans and layered top. "Looks like you've been having fun. Is there a bikini inside one of those bags?"

Her cheeks grew warm for no reason. "Yes, among other things."

"I hope you put everything on my account."

Reese shook her head. "Not today. Excuse me while I put them away."

He rubbed his hard jaw. "I don't know about you, but I haven't had dinner yet. Paul is going to drive us to Nolia's in Greenwich Village. The salmon and sea bass are to die for."

She bit her lip. He obviously needed to unwind after being with his in-laws. "Won't it make too long a day for Jamie?"

"He's staying in tonight. Rita, one of the maids who's been working here a long time, is going to take care of him while we're gone. I'm expecting her any minute."

Reese took a shaky breath. Going out to dinner with Nick alone wasn't part of her nanny job, but as the thought of turning down his offer entered her mind, she realized that she wanted to be with him so badly, she felt an ache to the palms of her hands.

"What should I wear?"

"Anything you feel like."

In other words, formal dress wasn't required. She was hot and sticky and needed a shower first.

"Don't take too long. I'm starving," he said in a husky tone.

She'd been hungry when she'd walked in the door, but with those words her stomach had too many butterflies to know what she was feeling. "I'll hurry."

Ten minutes later she joined him in the foyer wearing a sleeveless dress with a rounded neck in an allover black-on-white print. The summery outfit could be dressed up or down depending on her accessories. After brushing out her ponytail, she'd caught her hair back at the nape with a black chiffon scarf and slipped on low black heels.

When Nick saw her, the unmistakable glimmer in his eyes set a tone for the rest of the evening, making her feel feverish throughout their delicious dinner. A live jazz band prompted Nick to dance with her. He drew the eyes of every woman, young or old.

She thought of Cinderella, who got her chance to be spun around the castle ballroom with her prince. But in that childhood fairy tale, the author never described the feelings running riot inside the scullery maid who for one night had been transformed into a princess. The adult thoughts and desires of a woman weren't meant to be read by dreamy-eyed little girls.

Nick had told Reese he wanted her to experience some nightlife while she was in his employ. In her naïveté she'd given in to that temptation and thought she could handle it, but if he pulled her against his hard-muscled body one more time he'd feel her trembling.

"You're a wonderful dancer, Reese."

"Thank you. So are you."

"I could do this all night," he murmured near her ear.

Don't say another word, Nick. "If I hadn't walked around Macy's all afternoon, there's nothing I'd like more."

"I forgot about that. You should have said something sooner. We'll go."

Ever the consummate host who went out of his way to make her comfortable, they left the restaurant and rode back to the apartment in the limo. The maid was there to meet them.

"Jamie never made a peep."

"Thank you, Rita."

"Anytime." Her brown eyes flicked to Reese with interest before she left the penthouse.

When the door closed, Reese looked up at her incredibly handsome escort. "Thank you for a lovely evening, Nick. I must be the luckiest nanny in New York with the nicest employer and the sweetest little boy."

His eyes were veiled as he smiled at her. "We'll have to do it again."

No, no.

"Lest you've forgotten, Cinderella only had one night at the ball. It wouldn't do for the hired help to expect a repeat with the prince. Good night, Nick."

Reese left for her bedroom having meant what she'd said. To lose her head over this man when she was being paid to do a job for him would bring heartache—the kind she instinctively knew she would never recover from.

For the rest of the week she made certain she and Jamie were there to greet him when he walked through the door of the penthouse, but that was all. Once she'd told him about Jamie's day and answered any questions he had, she disappeared to get going on her studies.

On the following Friday she was studying on her laptop when she heard Jamie's distinct cry through the baby monitor. He hadn't built up to it. One minute it was quiet in the room. In the next, he'd let go as if he'd awakened with a nightmare, or was in pain.

He'd only been down for an hour since his one-o'clock bottle. She slid off the bed and rushed across the hall to the nursery. Alarmed to see him in so much distress, she picked him up to comfort him.

"Uh-oh—you're hot." She walked over to the dresser with him to get the thermometer. To date his health had been so perfect, she'd almost taken it for granted.

"Hmm...101.4. That's not good. Let's check to see what's going on." When she undid his stretchy outfit and diaper, she discovered he'd had diarrhea. "Oh—you've got a stomachache." She got him all clean again and put him in a fresh diaper and a shirt.

For the next hour she walked him around the

apartment on her shoulder, singing every song she could remember to comfort him. He remained restless and whimpered, then let out another heartrending cry before she felt him have another loose movement.

Back she went to the nursery and cleaned him up once more. This time she applied some rash cream so he wouldn't get sore. When she picked him up again, he burrowed into her neck, still feeling hot.

Without hesitation she carried him to her bedroom and phoned Nick on her cell. This was the first time she'd called him at his office since coming to work for him. Though she hated disturbing him, she knew he'd want to be told.

"Reese?" He picked up on the third ring. "Is there a problem?"

"I'm glad you answered. Jamie's come down with diarrhea and is running a temperature of 101. He's going to need fluids to lower it, but I'm not sure what the doctor would prescribe."

"I'll phone Dr. Wells right now. How long has Jamie been sick? When I left him this morning, he seemed fine."

"I know. He woke up crying in the middle of his afternoon nap. My sister Carrie uses Pedialyte when her baby gets dehydrated, so ask the doctor about that. Since we don't have any on hand, I'll give him some water for now."

"I'm on my way out the door," he declared in a decisive tone. "I'd planned to come home early anyway." Secretly she was relieved. Normally Nick hid his emotions well, but this was his little boy who was ill. He must be as nervous as she was, if not more so. "While you try to get more liquid down him, I'll call the doctor then stop by the drugstore."

"Good."

"I'll be home soon."

After she hung up, she went to the kitchen for a bottle and filled it with cool water. Jamie seemed eager enough to drink, but by the time she reached the nursery and fed him a little, he threw up.

She put him in the crib and changed his clothes for a second time. His temp had climbed another tenth of a degree. She wet a cloth and sponged his forehead and cheeks.

Before long Nick entered the penthouse. "Reese?"

"In the nursery."

As he came through the door, Jamie threw up once more. It frightened him so much he started crying harder. After she'd wiped off his mouth, Nick pulled him out of her arms and cuddled him against his chest. "Hey, sport—what happened to you?"

Her gaze fused with Nick's. "Did you reach the doctor?"

"His nurse said he'd call me back. In the meantime we're to try and get liquids down him in small increments."

"I've been doing that, but after a minute, up it comes. It must be some kind of flu."

"Maybe the Pedialyte will stay down." Nick kissed his forehead. "The nurse said it was good to use. I got him cherry. He's a lucky little guy you're here for him."

Nick was always ready to praise her. It made her want to do everything right in his eyes. "I'll take it to the kitchen and put some in a sterile bottle." When she returned to the nursery Nick told her the doctor had called. "We're to keep a close eye on him. If we can't get anything to stay down, we're to take him to emergency. The hospital will keep him informed."

She nodded. By evening he'd thrown up enough times to convince her this was serious. His temperature never dropped. "He seems too lethargic."

Lines marred Nick's face. "Let's take him to the hospital. I'll tell Paul to bring the car around."

"While you hold him, I'll put some things in the diaper bag for him."

In a short time they left the penthouse. Paul drove them to the E.R. entrance and they hurried inside with Jamie lying limp against his daddy's shoulder.

One of the emergency-room staff showed them to a cubicle. Right after that another person came inside the curtain. His tag said he was Dr. Marsh. He got to work checking the baby's vital signs. "How long has he been sick?"

Jamie didn't like being examined. His cries wrenched Reese's heart. "Since about two o'clock. It came on so fast I couldn't believe it. We've tried to get liquids down him, but he just spits it up and hasn't urinated for several hours."

"We'll have to culture him to find out if this infection is bacterial, but I'd say he's picked up Rotavirus."

"What is it exactly?" Nick's features had darkened in anxiety.

"A disease of the bowel that causes diarrhea and vomiting. Most children have had several incidences of it by the time they're five."

"How would he have gotten it?"

"It's transmitted several ways, but I would imagine your son picked it up through the air. Someone's cough could have spread it. It's highly contagious."

"I've heard it's serious—" Reese blurted.

"It can be when left untreated. If I'm right, we'll put him in isolation and hydrate him with an IV to bring back his body's salt and fluid levels to normal. He should get through this just fine."

Should? She and Nick shared a panicked glance.

"Who's your pediatrician?"

"Dr. Hebert Wells."

"In a minute a team will come in to take a blood sample. When we know for sure what we're dealing with, we'll call him. If it's bacterial, your doctor will treat him with an antibiotic."

Reese hugged her arms to her waist in agitation. "What more could we have done to have prevented this?"

The doctor eyed her with compassion. "As long as you're constantly washing your hands before and after you attend to your baby, that's pretty much all you can do." Jamie wasn't *her* baby, but she loved the sound of it.

"Reese has been very careful about that," Nick interjected. "I need to do it more often."

"Washing hands can prevent all kinds of illnesses."

Nick's lips tightened. "If an IV is called for, where will you insert it—he's so small?" He'd taken the question right out of her mouth.

"The IV team will decide, but probably in his foot. It hurts for a minute, but then it's over." Reese shared another worried glance with Nick.

"Go ahead and hold your baby until one of the staff shows you to the isolation area."

As the doctor left the cubicle, Nick reached for Jamie. Once he was back in his father's strong arms, he quieted down a little bit, but clearly he was miserable. Reese smoothed her hand over the back of his head. "You're all wiped out, aren't you, sweetheart."

"We're both here—" Nick talked to his son in a low, comforting tone "—and you're going to get feeling better soon."

Reese wanted to believe it, too, but she'd heard the underlying concern in his voice and was scared to death herself because the illness had robbed Jamie of his vitality.

In a minute someone came and took them through double doors to a restricted area where they were set up in a private room. Jamie cried some more. "I think he wants you, Reese." Nick handed the baby to her.

She hugged Jamie close and sang to him. The music kept him somewhat calm. When she lifted her eyes to Nick, she caught a look of such pain in his, it shattered her.

Something in his expression told Reese that Nick was thinking about his wife and how he'd lost her so quickly after they'd reached the hospital. In the two weeks she'd known Nick, he'd never talked about her except to explain how she'd died. Reese refused to consider the possibility that he was worrying his son would be taken from him, too, in so short a time.

"Nothing's going to happen to Jamie," she assured him with her heart in her throat. "You heard the doctor. Everyone's had Rotavirus in their lives. Even the two of us, and we're alive and healthy, right?" She flashed him a coaxing smile.

Reese wasn't destined to hear what he would have said back because two technicians came into the cubicle wearing masks. Jamie didn't like that and turned his head into her neck.

The taller one said, "If Mom and Dad will step outside the curtain, we'll get this over with quick." He reached for the baby Reese had to give up, but it killed her because Jamie cried out in protest.

"It's okay, sport," Nick assured him. "We'll be

right outside." He reached for Reese's hand and led her beyond the curtain. She knew he wasn't thinking as he drew her along with him, but a sensation of warmth traveled up her arm into her body. He didn't let go the whole time Jamie cried. With both their emotions raw, the feel of his hand gripping hers gave her the strength to deal with this crisis.

The technician had called them Mom and Dad. Right now she couldn't imagine feeling any different if Jamie were her son. She loved that baby with every fiber of her being.

All these years she'd planned for a career, not realizing what it meant to love a child like she loved Jamie. The bond with him was so strong, it tore her apart to think of leaving him right now. When the day came that she had children of her own, how would she be able to leave them?

What if she *were* his mother and had to get back to her job of running a company? She couldn't see it, not when Jamie needed her and Nick so desperately.

Together they stood having to endure his frightened cries. "For the last two weeks he's only been with the two of *us,*" she whispered. "He's not used to anyone else."

In a minute the team left and another masked team showed up with their cart. "Stay where you are. This won't take us long."

Nick squeezed her hand gently before letting it go. She presumed their arrival made him realize he'd been holding on to hers all that time. Reese wished he wouldn't have relinquished it. Without that physical connection, she was snatched back from her fantasy about being Jamie's mother. Nick had been part of that fantasy, too. The three of them, a family. How was she ever going to say goodbye to them when the time came?

Deep in turmoil, she heard the baby let out a yelping cry like the one she'd heard through the monitor. They'd just jabbed him, she was sure of it, the poor darling. In reaction she smoothed her hands nervously over jean-clad hips.

It had been hours since she'd looked in a mirror. At least her hair was back in a ponytail and not messy. When they'd left for the hospital, she'd been in too alarmed a state to think about changing out of the jade-colored T-shirt she'd put on to study. But none of that mattered with Jamie lying there feverish and sick.

"They're taking a hell of a long time in there," Nick muttered.

Reese bit her lip. "It seems that way to me, too."

"At this rate he's going to think he's been abandoned."

"But he won't remember once it's over."

"I'm not so sure of that." Something in his tone told her that wasn't idle talk. She wanted to ask him what he meant, but one of the team came outside the curtain with the cart, preventing further conversation.

"You can go back in now. We've attached his foot to a pad for protection. You can hold him all you want, just be mindful of the tubing."

She and Nick hurried back inside to rescue his howling child, but were met by the other technician. "Wash your hands first, then put on the sterile gloves from the container on the wall. After you've done that, wear the masks we've left on the counter. Do this every time you leave the cubicle for any reason until the doctor tells you if your baby has Rotavirus or not. Dispose of everything in the bin inside the bathroom here. Leave through the other door that leads into the hallway."

"Thank you," they both said at the same time.

Once they were alone, Reese urged Nick to wash first. "Jamie needs you." Though everything in her screamed to pick up the baby, he wasn't her son and it wasn't her place.

The warning Reese's mother had given her about not getting too attached to the baby had gone by the wayside the first time she'd laid eyes on Jamie. The beautiful boy had caught at her heartstrings. After meeting his father, Reese knew why. Now—after loving and playing with him over the past two weeks—there were so many heartstrings being pulled by both Wainwrights, she realized she was in terrible trouble.

Once they were washed, gloved and masked, they spent the next hour taking turns holding him while they tried everything to settle him down. Finally he fell asleep and Nick lowered him to the crib.

"He's not in pain right now, Nick."

"We can be thankful for that small mercy at least."

"You look exhausted. This is going to be an all-night vigil. Why don't you slip out and grab a bite to eat in the cafeteria first. When you come back, I'll go get something. I'd rather it was you he woke up to later."

Nick's eyes looked fierce above the mask. "He wants you just as much." Her heart pounded dangerously, but it wasn't from hunger or fatigue. "I don't know what we'd do without you."

She knew the waiting was getting to him, but the more he kept telling her that, the more she wanted to believe it. "Hurry, before he wakes up looking for you."

"All right, but I won't be long." He disappeared into the bathroom and shut the door. Reese walked over to the crib and looked down at the dear little boy she'd been privileged to take care of so far.

When Reese had helped her mom with her baby sister, she'd only been fourteen. Though she'd loved Emma, she couldn't compare the feelings and emotions that filled Reese now. Jeremy had riddled her with accusations about being a cold woman who put a career above the feelings a *normal* woman possessed.

If he could see into her heart and soul right now, he would discover Reese was more than normal, and Jamie wasn't even her son!

After consuming a sandwich and a piece of pie in record time, Nick left the cafeteria and walked outside the hospital doors. He had a phone call to make, but cell phones weren't permitted inside. His father-in-law answered.

"Nick?"

"Sorry to call you this late, Walter, but I thought you should know I won't be able to bring Jamie to White Plains tomorrow."

There was a long silence. "Anne predicted right about you."

He took a fortifying breath. "Jamie's in the hospital with a bad flu bug of some kind. They'll be keeping him overnight. Depending on what's wrong after the tests come back, he might be here tomorrow night, as well. I'll keep you posted and we'll plan to bring him to White Plains next weekend instead."

"What kind of flu?" Anne demanded. She'd picked up on another house phone the minute Walter had told her who was calling.

"We don't know yet."

"This never happened when he was with us."

Nick was sorry she'd come on the line. This was exactly what he'd hoped to avoid. "Every child gets it, Anne. The point is, he's receiving excellent care. I have to go back to him now. Tomorrow I'll let you know how he's doing. Good night."

He hung up. It was automatic for him to check his voice messages. To his surprise there was one from his father. While his parents were traveling, they never called him. Out of curiosity more than filial duty, he clicked on.

"Nicholas? This is your father." Nick shook his head because that was the way he always started out any phone call to him. The distance between them continued to widen. "Your mother and I are back on Long Island. I came in the office and discovered you'd already gone home.

Stan tells me you've got the boy with you at the penthouse. Why you would do that baffles me and could prove to be very unwise. We ran into the Ridgeways while we were vacationing in Cannes. They'll be back next week with their daughter Jennifer who's been staying with friends in England. She's a lovely young woman we want you to meet. Better not spring Jamie on her at first. You know what I mean. I expect a call from you before you go to bed."

Before I go to bed?

His father could say that when he never phoned for months at a time?

Nick clicked off. The pain he'd carried since he could first remember life kindled into white-hot anger. His parents could wait. Reese couldn't and neither could Jamie. He'd been gone too long as it was and hurried back to the E.R.

To his relief Jamie was still asleep. Reese's blue eyes, those mirrors of the soul, fastened on him with intensity. "The doctor still hasn't come back with the results."

"It's a busy night here. Why don't you go get something to eat now?"

"I will."

After she left through the bathroom, he washed his hands, then slipped on new gloves and a mask. Thankful his son was getting the rest he needed, Nick pulled up one of the chairs next to the crib to watch him.

He'd grown over the past couple of weeks. His father's question about why he would bring Jamie home to live could be answered by the baby lying right in front of him with an IV in his tiny foot.

This was why! There were changes going on every day of his son's life. Nick wanted to be in on all of them. No more chunks of time missing he could never get back.

Had his father or mother ever actually heard Nick say his first word or seen him take his first step? When Nick had gotten the flu as a baby, someone on the staff would have taken care of him. Nick's mother wouldn't have been able to tolerate being thrown up on. She would have left that to a nurse.

Reese on the other hand loved and kissed Jamie to death. That was her nature. Because of so much one-on-one attention, his son was blossoming.

You can't spoil a baby enough. Those were her words. Nick believed in her philosophy. Every baby should be so showered.

Nick's parents didn't have a clue. They'd been raised by nannies and their parents before them. His father's mention of the Ridgeway's daughter, another woman who had to be made in the express image of the other women in Nick's life, sickened him.

"Mr. Wainright?" Dr. Marsh had come in.

Nick got to his feet. "What's the verdict?"

"Your son has Rotavirus. I've talked to your pediatrician. He'll be by in the morning on rounds unless the baby's temp spikes. In the meantime we'll continue to do what we're doing and will come in at intervals to check his vitals. Do you have any questions for me?"

"Not that I can think of right now."

"If you and your wife need a cot, they're in the closet behind you."

"I appreciate you telling me that."

"This part of the hospital has been redone for the comfort of the parents."

"Whoever planned it must have had a baby here at one time."

"No doubt."

"For your information, my wife has passed away. Reese is the nanny."

Nick had to give Dr. Marsh credit for not reacting the way he probably would have under other circumstances. "You're lucky to have found someone who has a strong mothering instinct. That's going to help your son."

"I agree."

Reese returned soon after the doctor had left and washed her hands. "Do you know anything yet?"

He told her what he'd learned. She finished tying the mask and walked over to the crib. "I should think sleep is the very best thing for him."

"We're going to need it, too. It's after eleven." He went to the closet and pulled out the made-up cots, placing them end to end. There was enough room for the staff to move back and forth changing the IV while they did vitals and programmed their notes into the computer.

He heard a sigh. "Bed sounds good. Thank you for setting them up." She removed her sandals and slipped under the covers with her head at the far end. Maybe she'd done it on purpose so their heads couldn't possibly be close to each other. He was sorry about that, but at least they'd be spending the night in the same room with Jamie.

Nick shut off the overhead light. After studying his son for another few minutes, he took off his shoes and lay down on top of the cot, putting his hand behind his head. From his vantage point he could see her lying there on her side toward Jamie.

"Reese? Are you asleep yet?"

He watched her shift in the cot. "No. I know you're worried about Jamie, but he's getting the best care possible."

"I believe that, too. I just wanted to say that the reason I was so long was that I had to let Jamie's grandparents know he wouldn't be coming to White Plains in the morning."

"I'm sure they were upset."

Reese didn't know the half of it.

"Don't be surprised if they show up tomor-row."

"That would only be normal. In my family if anyone were in the hospital, a whole crowd would descend." Nick couldn't imagine what that would be like. "Too bad your parents are away and don't know he's ill."

"Actually they got back from Cannes today. I listened to my father's message on my voice mail."

"Are they coming over here tonight?"

"No. I didn't call him back."

A long silence ensued. "I see."

"You don't see at all, but you're so polite, you would never pry."

"Your personal life is none of my business."

"That's an excellent response."

"What do you mean?" She shot straight up in the cot. "I don't understand."

Just then one of the staff came in to check on Jamie. "How's he doing?" Nick asked as the nurse finished on the computer.

"His temp is up a little from before, but these

things take time. Try to get some sleep while he's quiet."

Nick's stomach clenched. There was no way he could do that right now. He got up from the cot and walked over to the crib. At this point Reese joined him.

"He's *got* to be all right, Nick!" He heard tears in her voice.

Without conscious thought he put his arm around her shoulders and pulled her to his side. After dancing with her last week, he needed her warm, curvaceous body next to his. Though she'd told him no more repeats, the fact that she didn't fight him right now revealed her deep need for comfort, too.

"What you said earlier," she whispered. "If I—"

"Forget it," he broke in. "I'm afraid I'm not myself tonight. We may be employer and nanny, but sometimes the lines get blurred. We've lived under the same roof for two weeks now. I find myself wanting to ask you questions I have no right to ask."

"I know what you mean." The tremor in her voice made its way through to his insides.

"So you admit you're a little curious about me."

"Of course." He noticed her hands cling to the edge of the crib. "I wouldn't be human otherwise."

"Go ahead and ask me why I haven't told my parents about Jamie being sick."

She bowed her head. "Not if you don't want to talk about it."

"Actually I do. You recall our conversation about my family being blue bloods? Well, I made a vow that Jamie's life is going to be different. Yes, he's a Hirst and a Wainwright, but I won't let him grow up under a system where appearances count for everything. That kind of life might be desirable at first, but it ends up destroying you."

"You feel like that's what happened to you?" she asked quietly.

"Our whole families have been destroying themselves for generations to the point that they don't have that human quality of giving and receiving affection. They don't feel it."

She looked up at him with eyes that were suspiciously bright. "But you're nothing like that!"

The impulse to crush her in his arms was so strong, he forced himself to let go of her altogether. "I was on my way to being exactly like that until a client made a chance remark three weeks ago that opened my eyes."

"What did he say?"

"He'd been offering his condolences and said there was nothing like a child to help you get over your loss. He obviously assumed I was the typical new father having to get up with him in the night for his feedings. But he didn't realize he was talking to a Wainwright who'd come from a cloistered, upper-class aristocracy.

"You can't imagine how I felt at that moment knowing Jamie was at my in-laws' being taken care of by their staff and I'd let it happen. Worse, my own parents saw nothing wrong with it. But the real crime was the one I'd committed by letting him go home with them in the first place.

By turning over my son's life to the hired help, I'd virtually abandoned him."

"But if you hated what your parents had done to you, then—"

"I know." He raked a hand through his hair. "It's complicated. At the time of Erica's death, everything was murky. But standing here now next to my son, I see things so clearly it terrifies me that I was once that other man.

"The truth is, I could have called my father back tonight and told my parents about Jamie, but they wouldn't have cared, and it wouldn't have occurred to them to come to the hospital. They've been emotionally absent from my life for thirty-four years. That's never going to change. My uncles, my cousins, they'll never change, either."

"Oh, Nick...I'm so sorry. I had no idea."

"How could you possibly know? You come from another world. A *real* world."

"At least Erica's parents have been there to support you."

"That's where you're wrong. They despise me."

"Because you hired me?"

"No, Reese. My problems with them stem back to a year ago when Erica agreed to a divorce."

"You divorced her?" She sounded shocked.

"Yes. We'd made one more stab at trying to patch up our two-year-old marriage, but it didn't work. It wasn't until after we separated that she told me she was pregnant. She moved back with her parents. I didn't see her again until I got a phone call that she was on her way to the hospital. You know the rest."

"So that's why there was no nursery at the penthouse."

"I let her have carte blanche decorating the apartment so she could entertain in style, but more often than not she stayed at White Plains. We lived apart much of the time, a situation that suited both of us. I know you can't comprehend that."

She kept her eyes averted. "It's just so sad."

"At the time it was simply the norm. When she died, I was devastated, but it was my guilt over our failed marriage that put me in a dark morass. I let them take the baby home. The problem is, Erica's parents believe that Jamie—and all the money that comes with him as my heir—belongs more to them than to me after I'd damaged the family pride. It was a case of 'it's just not done.'"

He heard a little moan come out of Reese.

"You sound horrified. A normal person would be. But in my world, I'd broken the code of our social mores by divorcing her and was viewed as a revolutionary. Letting her parents keep our son for a time would look good on the surface. My parents would prefer it if things stayed that way. Anything to preserve the image."

She shook her head. "How awful."

"I debated telling you all this. It's so messy and complicated and I'll understand if you don't want to involve yourself with it all. If you want to leave my employ, I'll give you a check for the full amount we agreed upon. But I would ask you not to leave until Jamie's on the mend."

Leave him and the baby?

If only Nick knew what Reese was really thinking. Though the day would come when she would have to go, she would never be ready to give up him or the baby.

She sucked in her breath. "Don't be ridiculous. The arrangement we made was that I wouldn't go until the end of the summer. If you're still in agreement, then let's not talk about it again."

Relief flooded her system when she heard him say, "Then we won't."

"Good. Right now your son needs us focusing on him and nothing else."

No sooner had she delivered her words than Jamie woke up crying. Nick hurried around to the other side of the crib to pick him up.

"Does he still feel as hot to you?"

His dark eyes flew to hers. "Yes."

That one word filled Reese with fresh alarm. Jamie's temperature had been elevated for close to eighteen hours now. The IV was supposed to be doing its job.

They took turns holding him. The minutes passed. Another nurse came in to check on him. She left without saying anything to them. That really frightened her. This went on for another half hour. Then Dr. Wells walked in the room already masked and gloved.

He gave them a quick glance. "Sorry to hear your son's been sick, Mr. Wainwright. Let me take a look at him."

While Nick handed the baby over, Reese stood back to watch the pediatrician, thankful he'd come. In a minute he lifted his head.

"I'm going to have you start feeding him some formula. The nurse will bring it to you. Just an ounce at a time. He might throw it up at first, but you persevere and we'll see if it finally stays down. I'll be back later."

The next hour was nightmarish with Jamie spitting up ten minutes after every ounce. She didn't know how Nick was holding up. He'd taken over because of love for his child. That was the way it should be.

She folded the cots back up and put them away so there was room for the chairs. When she sat down next to him and the baby, the sun had come up. Though the blinds were closed, light illuminated the room.

Reese checked her watch. "Nick—do you realize he hasn't thrown up for twenty minutes?"

His head lifted. "That's definite progress." He sounded elated.

"It *is!*" she cried.

The nurse came in a little while later. "How's he doing?"

"It's been a half hour since he last threw up."

"Terrific." She took the baby's temperature. "It's down four-tenths. I'll call Dr. Wells and tell him. Let him sleep now." She hurried out of the room.

Nick stood up and lay the baby back down in the crib.

Reese followed him over. "The worst must be over."

They both heard the door open and Dr. Wells came back in to examine the baby. "He's going to be fine. For the rest of the day give him formula when he seems ready for it. We'll keep the IV going. This evening I'll come by on rounds. If all is well, he'll be able to sleep in his own crib tonight."

"That's wonderful!" Reese cried as he left

the room. Luckily her mask muffled its full intensity.

Nick turned to her. His hands shot out to grasp her arms. "*You're* wonderful. I don't know what I would have done without you." Between his husky voice that sounded an octave deeper and those dark fringed eyes that were looking at her with such gratitude, she was overwhelmed by the feelings he engendered. But growing alongside her great happiness was a new fear clutching at her.

Last night he'd talked about the lines between nanny and employer getting blurred after living beneath the same roof. Try spending the whole night together in the same hospital room with the little baby they both adored.

This morning she couldn't find the lines anywhere.

CHAPTER SIX

"Is the diaper bag packed?"

"All done."

"Don't forget your new bathing suit."

Reese blinked. "We're going swimming?"

"We might."

"In your in-laws' pool?"

"Maybe. They have several."

She'd been swimming in the pool on the terrace every afternoon while Jamie was napping. He'd had a slight cold since they'd brought him home from the hospital last Saturday night, but Dr. Wells said it was to be expected. A week later Jamie was well and beaming. Next week she'd be able to move him around on top of the water and see how he fared.

"Ready?" he called out.

"Just about."

While he was moving around in the apartment,

she hurried back to her bedroom and stashed the new suit inside her purse. After breakfast she'd gotten dressed for the drive to White Plains. She'd chosen to wear a rose-colored sundress with a white, short-sleeved bolero jacket. It was a step up from jeans, more presentable for a nanny who was about to face the Hirsts again. A white ribbon for her ponytail to match her sandals, and she left the bedroom.

"Let's go!"

After putting the freeze pack with the milk into the diaper bag, Reese met him in the foyer. Nick had dressed in cargo pants and a tan crew neck shirt. Even though he'd shaved, there was that hint of dark shadow that gave him a slightly disreputable look, adding to his sensuality. The sight of him looking beyond handsome with his wavy black hair and the relaxed look on his face took her breath.

She quickly switched her gaze to his son strapped in his carryall. Nick had put him in his white outfit with the tiger on the front. The baby was three months and a week old now. He was bigger and looked so healthy you would never have guessed he'd been ill a week ago. Unable to resist, she kissed his cheek several times. His little mouth curved into a smile that reminded her of Nick. It turned her heart right over.

She tickled his tummy. "We're going on a trip in our favorite rocket ship." She sang the song one of her friend's four-year-old loved. Jamie loved it, too.

He laughed out loud, provoking a grin from Nick. His gaze found hers. "You sound happy."

"Who wouldn't be? When I think of last week…"

"Don't remind me."

They left the apartment. Soon they'd climbed in the limo and were headed out of the city under a semicloudy sky, but nothing could dim her elation at being able to spend the whole day with Nick and Jamie.

Since that night in the hospital when he'd told her about his background and failed marriage, she wasn't as nervous to meet Erica's parents. Forewarned helped her to be forearmed.

Nick's decision to break from tradition and bring on the condemnation of two families had been made because of his love and need of Jamie. It took an incredibly strong man of amazing character to do what he did. It couldn't have been easy and she didn't envy him having to deal with his in-laws today. For that reason Reese intended to be his support.

In some way things had been easier since the hospital. The bonding that had taken place with Jamie made everything they did seem more natural when the three of them were together. Nick had come home around four every afternoon. She understood his need to spend as much time as possible with his son.

Reese felt as if the penthouse had become a happy place for Nick. Nothing could mean more to her when she realized how much of his past had been marred by the weight of a painful childhood as well as a difficult marriage. Nick still hadn't told her all that had gone on between him and Erica to drive them apart, but then Reese was only the nanny. Every once in a while she had to remember that, but it was getting harder and harder.

On this trip she sat next to Jamie, who loved his

pacifier and blue rattle. With Nick sitting straight across from the baby, he could talk to him and keep him entertained, but it was Jamie who entertained them. Every time he laughed, his pacifier fell out and Nick put it back in. Jamie thought it was a game and kept doing it. Maybe he was too little to realize what was going on, but it was hilarious and they laughed all the way to White Plains.

When they came in sight of the Hirst estate, Reese understood even more the dividing line that separated people with lifestyles like Nick's and his former wife's from the rest of the world. They drove past a sign indicating public parking around the west side of the two-story mansion. Paul took the tree-lined driveway to the front entrance and helped Reese out with the diaper bag. Nick followed with Jamie and the three of them started up the steps. By the time they reached the front door, Walter Hirst had opened it. The older man couldn't hide his surprise at seeing Reese.

"We're in the dayroom."

If it had been Reese's father who'd opened the door, the first thing he would have said was something like, "There's my grandson! Come here and say hello to your old granddad." He would have reached for the baby and walked him through their house to show Grandma.

Reese had thought she was prepared for this, but even with the explanations Nick had given her, to see and feel the continued lack of personal warmth and affection coming from Erica's father disturbed her.

The interior of the mansion might be an architectural triumph of nineteenth-century elegance, but the only life Reese could see came from Jamie, whose head kept turning as they followed Mr. Hirst to a room with a surprising contemporary decor. His grandmother, wearing a stylish two-piece suit in lime-green, was just walking through the doors leading in from a beautiful flower garden Reese could see beyond her.

"We didn't expect you this early. I take it Jamie's better now."

"He's fine," Nick stated. "In fact you're perfect, aren't you, sport." He kissed his cheeks while he undid the straps and lifted him out. "You'll notice he's grown."

"Put him down in the carriage."

With no playpen or swing, Nick had little choice unless he wanted to plop Jamie in his grandmother's arms. But she gave no indication that she wanted to hold him. Reese knew there were many people in the world who couldn't show affection, no matter their social class. Still, this was Jamie's family and it just didn't seem natural.

Now that she thought about it, a hint of Nick's rebellion had come out when he'd shown them the nursery and deposited Jamie in her arms. Today he held back and abided Anne's wishes.

The trouble with a carriage was that it blocked part of the view for the baby, who started crying as soon as Nick moved out of his line of vision. Reese's first instinct was to take him right out. Like Nick, she, too, had to hold back from grabbing him.

"I brought this." Reese set the diaper bag down on one of the chairs. "It has enough bottles and diapers for today."

"We have everything he'll need. Walter? Will you tell the nurse they're here." Jamie was not happy and his cries were getting louder.

"I'll be back for him at six." Nick flicked Reese a glance. "Let's leave them alone, Ms. Chamberlain."

They walked out the mansion through the front door with Jamie's cries still following them. She assumed he meant they were going to explore the estate and go swimming later on. To her shock Nick headed for the limo and helped her inside.

She stared at him in puzzlement. "I thought our plan was to stay close by. What if Jamie needs you?"

"Then he'll cry his heart out until he falls asleep."

"Nick..."

His grim expression was too much. The past week had been so carefree, Reese could hardly bear to see his brooding expression come back. "I didn't have a choice, Reese, because I made them a promise. But after today, all promises are off."

He flicked on the intercom. "Paul? Drive us to the heliport."

"Where are we going?" she asked when he'd finished.

"Out on my sailboat."

Her heart thudded with sickening speed. "If we need a helicopter, it must be pretty far away."

"Don't worry. We're only going to Martha's Vineyard outside Edgartown. One of our summer homes is there."

A summer home there, an estate with horses on Long Island, a penthouse on Park Avenue, a villa in Cannes. Reese had an impression those possessions only constituted the tip of an enormous iceberg. If Jamie didn't have a daddy who'd decided to break the cycle of emotional neglect that went with so much luxury, he could be suffocated by it all the way Nick had been.

He studied her for a moment. "Have you ever been sailing?"

She knew it was his favorite sport. "No. One time our family went to Wisconsin and we crossed Lake Michigan on the ferry in choppy conditions. None of us did well. That's the sum total of my knowledge of being on water."

A light gleamed in his eyes. "As long as you can swim, that's all I need to know. When we get out beyond where the breeze fills the sail, you'll find out you're a wonderful sailor."

"That's wishful thinking. I only hope I won't be imitating Jamie's bout of last weekend."

He chuckled. "You don't have the flu."

Reese knew Nick wanted and needed this outing, if only to take his mind off leaving Jamie with his grandparents. *Please don't let me get seasick.* When she saw the helicopter, another prayer went up about not getting airsick. She'd never been on one of those, either.

In the end she needn't have worried because Nick's cell phone rang before they even exited the limo. After he picked up, his gaze sought hers. She tried to read his expression as he listened to the person on the other end. It went on for a minute. After he hung up, he told Paul to turn the limo around and go back.

Her brows lifted. "Jamie?"

"He won't settle down. Anne says the nurse can't do anything with him, so if she can't, that's it."

Reese bit her lip. "I was afraid of that. Jamie worships you." She bet Nick's mother-in-law told him it was the nanny's fault for spoiling him and probably decried Nick ever removing Jamie from their house in the first place.

"Nothing could please me more," he declared in a satisfied voice. "Now we can take him with us. I'll call ahead for a cooler of food and drinks to be packed for us."

The burst of elation exploding inside Reese only lasted until she remembered her mother's last question to her. *"You've got a terrific head on those shoulders and broke off with Jeremy for a reason. I don't have to worry about you losing sight of your career plans just yet, do I?"* Not for the first time, Reese had to remind herself that she was just the temporary nanny. But the pain she felt at the thought of leaving this little family was becoming too much.

When they reached the mansion, Reese could hear Jamie's heart-wrenching sobs from the foyer of the mansion. They hurried down the hall to the dayroom and found the nurse pacing the floor with him. His in-laws stood around looking upset.

"Hey, sport? What's going on?" Nick walked

over to the distraught-looking woman and took the baby from her arms. Jamie caught sight of his daddy and lunged for him before bursting into another paroxysm of tears. Reese could almost hear him saying, 'Why did you leave me?'

When he burrowed his head into the side of Nick's neck, Nick must have felt it deep in his heart. In a few seconds peace reigned. While Jamie clung to him, everyone in the room looked infinitely relieved.

"I think there's been enough excitement for one day. Why don't you come to the penthouse next weekend and we'll try this again."

"We'll be in Salzburg. Don't you remember?" Anne sounded indignant. "You and Erica went with us two years ago."

"I'm sorry. This new job of parenting has taken over my life. Call me when you're back and we'll make arrangements. Have a safe trip."

Jamie refused to leave his arms, so Reese picked up the carryall and diaper bag before they headed for the limo waiting outside the mansion. Once Nick got in the backseat with him, Reese's eyes zeroed in on the baby.

"Your cute little face is all splotchy from crying. Here's your pacifier. Do you want your rattle, too?"

His fingers glommed right on to it. He didn't fight Nick as he strapped him in the infant car seat.

"Crisis averted," he said to Paul before the older man shut the door. In seconds they were off.

Her eyes flew to Nick's. "That wasn't a pleasant moment back there."

"No, and there's not going to be another one like it again."

She covered Jamie's face with kisses until she got a smile out of him. "You're so worn-out, you'll probably sleep all the way."

Reese didn't realize how prophetic her words would be. He slept through the fabulous helicopter flight that took them to the famous little island off Cape Cod. They were set down at Katama Airpark only a few miles from Edgartown.

Nick took them to one of the harbor restaurants where they ate a delicious shrimp lunch. Afterward they walked around the historic part of the town and visited some of the shops. It wasn't until they reached the boat dock on the Wainwright's property that the baby's eyes fluttered open. He'd missed everything.

Reese found it so funny, she started to laugh. Nick joined in. He was still smiling when he transferred his son from the ramp onto the end of the immaculate, twenty-three-foot sailboat called the *Aeolus*.

"What does it mean?" she asked him.

"In Greek mythology, Aeolus was the god of the winds."

"That's beautiful." The white keel had a blue stripe. She thought of the little boat she'd bought for Nick and couldn't wait for him to open his present, but she'd put it off until after they'd finished sailing.

Excitement mounted in Reese to see all the boats out on the water. This was a day out of time, one to treasure before they went back to the city. But having Jamie with them was the reminder she needed to remember she was his nanny, nothing else.

Nick brought out two adult life vests and an infant life jacket. While he went about getting the boat ready and undoing ropes, she laid Jamie down on one of the benches and changed his diaper. He loved being bare and kicked his strong legs as if he was doing exercises. She laughed with pure pleasure before putting a fresh diaper on him.

With him propped against her shoulder, she went down to the galley. There was a microwave so she could warm his bottle. By the time she climbed the stairs with him, Nick had everything ready to go. She put the bottle down. Together they helped put Jamie's infant vest on, but she was unbearably aware of Nick and his potent masculinity. Their hands brushed, sending rivulets of yearning through her.

He kissed his boy's tummy before snapping everything in place. "I know you don't like it, sport, but that's the rule." He fastened him back in his carryall. "You'll get used to it."

With a speed that took her breath, Nick's gaze unexpectedly flicked to hers. "Now it's *your* turn." The message in his dark brown eyes was unmistakable. They traveled over her features and down her body, melting her from the inside out. She got this heavy sensation in her legs. Her hands felt pains that traveled up her arms.

His male mouth was like a vortex drawing her in. Thrilled and terrified because her desire for him was so palpable he had to know it, she put out her hands to take the vest from him so he wouldn't touch her. Instead his hands closed over hers, pulling her against him, sending a paralyzing warmth through her body.

"I'm going to kiss you, and I very much hope that you won't fight me."

She couldn't have if she'd wanted to. From the moment she'd climbed in the back of the limo and had discovered a man who surpassed her every notion of the ultimate male, she'd wanted *him*. It was that simple, and that impossible, but right now she couldn't remember the reason why and didn't want to.

In the next breath he found her softly parted mouth. Incapable of doing anything else, she melted against him and let herself go, craving the taste of him as he took their kiss long and deep. Oh… She'd never felt sensations like this in her life. He drew her closer in a quick compulsive movement. The vest fell to her feet, but she was barely cognizant.

It came as a shock to realize his hunger matched hers, sending fire licking through her veins. Reese felt the low groan way down in his throat before it permeated her body. As it reached her inner core, her helpless cry drew a response of refined savagery from him.

"You couldn't possibly know how beautiful you are." A fever of ecstasy consumed her with each insistent caress of his lips on her face, her hair, her throat. "I want to take you below," he whispered against her lips, swollen from the passion they shared. "If I've shocked you, I've shocked myself more."

She took an unsteady breath and eased herself out of arms that were slow to relinquish her. The slight rocking of the boat didn't help her equilibrium. "What's really shocking is that I'd like to go downstairs with you," she admitted because total gut honesty was required right now.

"But after I broke off with Jeremy, I made a promise I wouldn't let anything get in the way of my goals. A man can make you lose focus. Who knows what could happen to me after a glorious day on the ocean in your arms. I—I know it would be wonderful," she stammered, "because I've just had a taste of you and crave more."

Nick's eyes narrowed on her mouth. He might as well have started kissing her again. She had to look away or she'd fling herself back into his arms.

"Your honesty is another quality about you I admire." Out of the periphery she watched his hard body lounge against the side of the boat. "What happened between you and Jeremy?"

"Probably the kind of thing that went wrong with you and Erica." She'd reached the tipping point and needed distance from this man who'd caused her world to reel.

Jamie wasn't fussing yet, but she knew his hunger had been building. She pulled him out of his carryall, then sat down and settled him in her arms to feed him.

"You mean you allowed yourself to drift into your engagement?" he asked in a benign tone.

Her head flew back. "Is that what happened to you?" she asked before she realized how revealing that question must have sounded. All along she'd been thinking Erica had to have been his grand passion because he could have had any woman he wanted.

"Why don't we concentrate on you and Jeremy first."

"He's not in my life anymore."

"Humor me anyway," he insisted.

"Well, we met at the bank where my father does business. That was the summer before I started at Wharton. We fell in love and dated until I went away, then we relied on emails and phone calls until we could be together. I went home at every vacation opportunity. He came to see me twice.

"Last fall he asked me to marry him and gave me an engagement ring. He knew I didn't want to get married before graduation, but when I went home at Christmas, he wanted to be married right away. No more waiting.

"I told him I would, but that we'd have to live apart while I was still away at school. That's when he gave me an ultimatum. Either I marry him before the end of the month and stay in Lincoln, or we break up."

The baby had finished his bottle. She pulled a receiving blanket out of the diaper bag and put it over her shoulder to burp him.

"I thought I knew him, but I didn't. It finally came out that he didn't want a working wife. He made enough money and wanted me to stay home so we could start a family. I told him I wanted children one day, but my education and work came first.

"I was amazed that my scholarship to Wharton meant nothing to him. He had a finance degree and aspirations to rise to the top, but didn't take mine seriously. It's too bad he didn't realize I meant what I said. It would have saved us both a lot of pain. I gave him back his ring and told him goodbye."

"Have you seen him since?"

"No."

"He's probably still waiting for you to change your mind."

"Then he's waiting in vain."

In the silence that followed, Nick reached for his life vest and put it on. Clearly he considered this conversation over. She'd learn nothing more from him about his marriage because he'd come out here to sail.

After their brief, intimate interlude that could have ended in her making the most disastrous mistake of her life, he was ready to head out to sea, the rapture of the moment forgotten. She had the gut feeling that the invitation to join him below wouldn't happen again on this trip or any other trips he planned in the future.

If he thought she was still feeling needy after her broken engagement and that's why she'd been an ardent participant in what they'd just shared, then let him go on thinking it. She didn't want him knowing her guilty secret.

To have fallen in love with her employer went against all the rules of being a nanny, but that's what she'd done. She was madly in love with Nick Wainwright. Between him and his son, she would never be the same person again.

No one could tell her Erica Hirst hadn't been desperately in love with him, too. You couldn't be in his presence five minutes without wanting any love he was willing to give. If anyone had *drifted* into a permanent relationship—if that's what had really happened—it would have been Nick.

Erica must have been shattered when he'd asked her for a divorce. Reese wanted to believe that the knowledge she was pregnant with Nick's child had brought her some solace in spite of her grief. If Reese had been in her shoes, she knew she would have grieved over losing Nick.

How tragic that she'd died. Tears pricked her eyelids. She loved their beautiful boy with all her heart.

"Reese?" His voice had a deep, grating quality. "Are you all right? I didn't mean to dredge up your pain."

Maybe it was better he thought Jeremy was the source of her distress, but nothing could be further from the truth. She shook her head. "You didn't. I thought you and I were having a simple conversation. Naturally our pasts would come up." She put the baby back in his carryall. "I think your son is on the verge of falling asleep again. Where shall we put him while we're out sailing?"

"Keep him right next to you. I'll do all the

work, but put on your life vest first." He handed it to her.

Back to square one, the place where she'd gotten too physically close to Nick and had given in to her longings. Not this time around!

She slipped it on and fastened the straps.

"Are you ready?"

Reese nodded.

He walked to the rear of the boat and started the motor at a wakeless speed. Slowly they headed toward the water beyond the buoys. Once past them, he cut the motor and raised the white sail. A light breeze filled it and then there was this incredible rush of sensation as the boat lifted and skimmed across the water. She found it wasn't unlike the feeling of Nick kissing her senseless.

When she was an old woman, all she would have to do was close her eyes and remember the sight of the gorgeous, powerfully built man at the helm with the wind disheveling his black hair. For a little while she would relive being crushed in his arms and invited to visit paradise with him. That kind of joy only came once.

She dreaded for the day to be over, but the

time came when Nick had to take them back to the port. Twilight had fallen all around them. After they'd floated alongside the pier and he'd jumped out of the boat to tie the ropes, she rummaged in the big diaper bag for the gift-wrapped package.

While he was still down on his haunches, she handed it to him.

"What's this?"

"It'll be Father's Day in a few hours. Before Jamie fell asleep, he asked me to give this to you. He told me to tell you he had the most wonderful day of his life out here with his daddy."

A stillness surrounded Nick before he undid the paper and discovered the sailboat. In the semi-darkness his white smile stood out. He turned it this way and that. "The *Flying NJ?*"

"Yes. A Nick and Jamie partnership. He thought you might like to put it on your desk at work."

"*Reese...*" He stepped back in the boat. With his hand still holding his gift, he cupped her chin with the other, lifting her face to his gaze. "No one ever gave me a present like this before."

"That's because it's your first Father's Day and

your son isn't very old yet," she teased to cover the intensity of her emotions.

He brushed his mouth against hers, melting her bones. "Where did you come from, Ms. Chamberlain?"

"The East 59th Street Employment Agency."

"My secretary did good work picking you. I'm going to have to give her a bonus."

"I'm glad she picked me, too. Jamie's...precious." Her voice caught before she moved away from him. She was in danger of begging him to take her below. If that happened, then a whole night alone with him would never be enough.

CHAPTER SEVEN

Two weeks later Reese entered the apartment building with Jamie after an afternoon of walking and shopping. The concierge called to her. "You have mail, Ms. Chamberlain."

She saw a postcard from Rich Bonner, his fourth, forwarded from the post office in Philadelphia to her temporary address here. His persistence irritated her. There was also a letter from Wharton. The school was no doubt reminding her of the test coming up in two weeks. She'd registered for it and would be taking it online.

"Thank you, Albert."

Once she'd tucked the mail in the sack, she went on up to the penthouse. Before she read anything, she had something more important to do. Jamie would be four months old in another week, but she couldn't wait for his birthday.

Her sister had one of those fold-out colorful

quilts with the ends of a mobile sewn in. When you opened it and set it on the floor, the mobile sprang open. The baby would lie there on his back entertained with all kinds and colors of small blocks and shapes and mirrors dangling above him. When she'd been walking through the toy store, she saw one like it and had to buy it.

"You're going to love this," she told Jamie as she wheeled him down the hall to her bedroom. As soon as she washed her hands, she pushed him through to the nursery and changed his diaper in his crib. She left him long enough to wash her hands again, then hurried back.

The little Tigger clock she'd bought for him last week said it was five after four. Nick would be home any minute. She lived for this time of the day when he walked through the front door and said he was home. Today was Friday, which meant he'd be home for the whole weekend.

He was always the perfect employer, but since their outing on the boat when she'd come so close to making love with him, he hadn't touched her and the deprivation was killing her.

"Come on, sweetheart." She picked up the baby, pouring out all her love on him. "You're getting heavier, do you know that?" With a kiss, she knelt down on the floor with him where she could place him under the mobile on his back.

"There." A red ladybug hung from a coil so you could pull on it. She put it in his hand. His fingers tried to crush it and it sprang away. Reese laughed and put it in his hand again, thus commencing a game that had them both laughing. She was so involved, she didn't realize Nick had come in the room until he'd gotten down on the floor with them.

"This looks so fun I think I'll try it myself." His hip brushed against hers as he put his head inside to kiss his son.

Jamie was overjoyed to see his father. In the excitement his hands knocked several objects so they swung. Reese was so excited to feel Nick's body next to her, she almost forgot to breathe.

His deep laughter rumbled through her, enchanting her. When he backed out, he suddenly pulled Reese closer so she was half lying on top of him with her face over his.

"A man could get used to looking up when there's so much to entice him." He undid the ribbon on her ponytail and her hair cascaded around her face. "I've been wanting to do this for weeks."

It was his fingers twining in her hair that opened the floodgates. With no immunity against the intensity of his desire, Reese couldn't help but lower her mouth to his, aching for the assuagement only he could give.

With slow deliberation he began to devour her. His breath was so sweet, so familiar, her senses swam. They kissed as if obeying some primitive rhythm. His lips traveled to the scented hollow of her throat. "You smell divine, do you know that? You feel divine."

"So do you." She let out a small gasp because the pressure of his mouth had changed, becoming so exquisite and loving, she would have fainted from pleasure if she weren't already on the floor with him.

He rolled her over on her back and kissed her passionately again and again until she couldn't tell where one kiss left off and another one began.

Caught up in a euphoria such as she'd never known, she had no idea what time it was or how much time had passed until Jamie started to make hungry noises. Good heavens, the baby—

"He can wait for his bottle one more minute, or two, or three," Nick said in a voice raw with emotion, pressing another hot kiss to her mouth, each one growing more urgent than the last.

Reese agreed as she gave in to the needs building inside her. His charisma had drawn her to him from the start, but now it was his sheer, potent male sensuality that had ensnared her. The slight rasp of his jaw brought out a wanton side in her she didn't know she possessed. His hunger, never satisfied, was making her feel immortal.

Only Jamie's cries becoming louder had the power to bring her back to earth. "Nick—"

His answering groan of protest meant he'd been brought back, too. She felt his hard-muscled body roll away. Reese caught a glimpse of dark eyes glazed with the heat of their passion before he got to his feet.

She looked around, surprised to see his suit jacket and tie on the floor. He had to have discarded them in a hurry after he'd walked in. Reese lowered her head. What had she done? What was she doing?

Nick left the room with Jamie to get him a bottle. By the time she got to her feet, her body couldn't stop throbbing. She was completely dazed by emotions and feelings that had overwhelmed her. In a way it really frightened her. Nick had the power to take away her heart, soul, mind, will, *everything*—without even trying.

But it was *her* fault, not his. There was no force involved with him. All he had to do was touch her or say something and she was incapable of denying him or walking away. To do that, she would have to break her contract. But giving up Jamie would break her heart and leave Nick in a crisis until he found another nanny.

You've gotten yourself in a terrible mess, Reese.

In a druggedlike stupor, she picked up the sack and almost threw it away before she remembered the mail inside it. After pulling it out, she tossed the bag in the wastebasket and looked at the postcard first. Laguna Beach.

Hey, beautiful— Wish you were here surfing with me. There are some waves rolling in with your name on them. By any chance did you get a letter from Wharton?

Reese stared at the unopened envelope in her hand.

I got one the other day. Email me either way, okay? Hope you are ready for the exam! Ciao for now. Rich.

She had no intention of contacting him, but she did have to admit she was curious about his mention of a letter. He wouldn't have said anything if all that was in it was the reminder of the exam coming up.

Nick must have carried Jamie out to the terrace to feed him. Thankful he'd disappeared to give her time to gather her wits, she wasted no time opening the letter. It was from the dean of her department no less.

Dear Ms. Chamberlain:
Two students whose academic achievement has set them above the rest of their graduating class have been given coveted internships for

the coming fall semester. It is my privilege to inform you that you are one of those two remarkable scholars.

Congratulations, Ms. Chamberlain, on your outstanding record. I am proud and pleased to tell you that you have been placed with Miroff and Hooplan located on Broadway in New York City, as an analyst. You'll do research and make books, but more detailed information will be forthcoming from my office shortly.

I wanted you to receive this letter in plenty of time to find living accommodations and plan your finances accordingly.

Again may I express my personal satisfaction over your stellar performance here at Wharton. Miroff and Hooplan will be fortunate to have you.

Best Regards.

Reese pressed the letter to her chest. Miroff and Hooplan was on the top-ten list of brokerage companies in the nation. She couldn't believe it. This truly was a dream come true.

Was it the dean Mrs. Tribe had talked to when she'd been checking on Reese's background?

As for Rich, his question meant he'd received the other internship. She wondered where he would be working. All she had to do was email him and she'd find out. Maybe it was uncharitable, but she hoped it wasn't next door or across the street from Miroff and Hooplan!

Though an internship meant being on call 24/7 as a grunt, she would be a grunt in an exclusive brokerage house. She felt a shiver of excitement run thorough her. She read the letter over again. Her parents needed to hear about this. They'd loved and supported her all these years so that she could realize her dream. She owed them for many things, but especially for their belief in her ability to succeed. Now would be a good time to reach her mother.

After moving the quilt mobile away from the crib, she left the nursery for her bedroom to make the call.

"Where are *you* going in such a hurry?" Reese had been moving so fast, she'd almost run into Nick in the hall. Jamie was resting against his broad shoulder. After the way she'd lost it in his arms, she could hardly look at him yet without blushing or feeling the strong passion between them again. "When I stopped for my mail, Albert told me you received some, too. By the rate of your speed leaving the nursery, it must be important."

Nothing got past Nick. Nothing.

"Something from Jeremy maybe?"

Jeremy—

After kissing Nick as if her very life depended on it, her ex-fiancé had been so far from her mind, she'd forgotten he existed. Reese struggled for breath. On a burst of inspiration, she handed him the letter. She needed to prove to herself as well as to him that no matter how attracted she was to him, she was still on the path to forging a place for herself in the business world.

She felt the full force of his penetrating gaze before he scanned the contents. As she watched him, his demeanor began to change. He'd been so certain this was about her ex-fiancé.

When he lifted his eyes, she saw an expression of incredulity stamped across his striking features. "I knew you were a student, but I had no idea you were the caliber of scholar to have earned this kind of entrée into Miroff's."

"The letter came as a complete surprise to me," she said in a quiet voice. "I was about to phone my parents with the news."

There was a pause before he said, "When you asked me about the stock market, I understand now that it was no idle question." He didn't sound accusing exactly, but he didn't sound himself, either. She couldn't decipher his reaction.

"It wasn't an in-depth question, either." Reese felt strange having to explain herself to him. Until now there'd never been this void between them. She didn't understand it.

"Jeremy really didn't know the real you, did he."

Jeremy again. Why did Nick sound so cold? That was the only word that came close to describing his response. Anger or rudeness she might have tolerated, but this aloof side of him was something new. If they could just get on a better footing.

"Can I do anything for you or Jamie?"

He shook his dark head. "Now that I'm home, you're free for the weekend."

To hear him say that in an almost wintry tone of voice was like being banished to the outer darkness. This was pain in a new dimension. For once she didn't dare kiss Jamie.

"Before I forget, your house phone rang this morning. I picked up so it wouldn't waken the baby. Someone named Greg called, but he didn't leave a message. About an hour later a man named Lew phoned wanting to speak to you. When he realized you weren't here, he said he'd catch up with you at the Yacht Club tonight. If you need me to watch Jamie, I—"

"I don't," he broke in, "but I appreciate the offer." He handed her back the letter. When she took it, the postcard fell out of her hand. Nick grabbed it up before she could. If he'd looked for Jeremy's name before returning it to her, then he would be disappointed.

Summoning all her strength, she picked herself up off the ground mentally and smiled. "If something should change, I'll be in my room studying."

"For what exactly?"

"The G7 and G65." He knew what they were. Once upon a time he'd had to study for them, too. "My exam is coming up before the end of the month."

"I have no doubt you'll crush it." Why was there that glitter in his eyes? Just a little while ago they'd been glazed with desire.

"We'll see."

The quilt mobile Reese had bought for Jamie was another hit out of the ballpark. Nick sat in the rocking chair and leaned forward, watching his son play beneath it. All the objects stimulated him so much, it took him a long time before he fell asleep. That suited Nick, who needed time to wind down before he exploded with emotions so foreign to him, he didn't know himself anymore. This was Leah's doing.

—*I've found someone I believe will suit you and the baby.*

—*As long as she likes children and is a real motherly type and not some cardboard creation, I bow to your wisdom. Tell me more about her.*

—You once told me you prefer to attack a new project without listening to any other voices first while you form your own opinion. I think that's a good philosophy, especially in this case.

This case meaning a young woman who played dual roles to perfection.

Nick bit down hard. Reese had wanted a job that only lasted three months and she'd meant it! Jeremy-whatever-his-name was a fool for not having realized he'd never been in the running for the long haul.

But now that Nick had taken the time to calm down, he realized his anger at Jeremy had been misplaced. The fault lay in himself for assuming he could talk Reese into staying on as his nanny longer than just the summer. When he thought of her leaving now, he couldn't handle it.

Filled with fresh panic, he pulled out his cell and called his secretary.

"Nick? I'm glad you phoned. Greg, Lew and your father have been trying to reach you. He told me to tell you the time for the Yacht Club party tonight has been changed from six-thirty to seven. I left the message on your voice mail."

"Thank you." He shot out of the rocking chair and wandered through the joining door to his bedroom. "Leah? How many women did you interview for the nanny position?"

"Four. Does this mean Ms. Chamberlain isn't working out?"

His hand almost crushed his phone. "She's working out very well, but I'm thinking of the future."

"What happened to the Cosgriffs' nanny?"

"Nothing that I know of, but I've decided I don't want her to come."

"Would you like me to start looking again?"

"Not quite yet, but I am curious. How many applied?"

"I believe Mr. Lloyd said they had five hundred and forty applications on hand."

Considering the state of the economy, he shouldn't have been surprised. "How did you tell him to screen them?"

"I asked him to pick out the ones with the highest education."

He rubbed the back of his neck in surprise. "That was it?"

"Yes. Those with undergraduate degrees or higher still wanting to take a nanny job for only three months would have something else going on in their brain. When he gave me the four names, I started making calls, checking references.

"One of Ms. Chamberlain's professors told me she had a spark of genius in her. That was a plus. She came from a family with five siblings and was the youngest applicant of the four, which I felt was another point in her favor. You have to be able to move quick and get down on the floor with a baby."

A wave of heat flooded Nick's system when he remembered what he'd been doing on the nursery floor with her less than two hours ago.

"What tipped the scales in her favor?"

"You mean you haven't found that out yet?"

Another layer of heat poured off him. Leah knew him too well. They had few secrets. One thing he could count on was her honesty.

"Did you know she was given an internship as an analyst at Miroff and Hooplan for the fall?"

"Well, I'll be damned. Good for her."

Nick had found out all he needed to know. "Talk to you later. And Leah—"

"Yes?"

"Thank you."

Before Jamie woke up, Nick needed to do damage control.

Reese had changed into white cargo pants and a khaki blouse. When she heard the knuckle rap, she was on her way out with no destination in mind. She'd lived through a tumult of emotions this afternoon and needed to walk until she dropped.

Grabbing her purse, she opened the door. Nick stood there without Jamie, his arm braced against the doorjamb. She braved his penitent gaze and felt her heart thud because the darkness she'd felt from him earlier seemed to have gone.

He studied her with relentless scrutiny, as if looking for some sign that he might be welcome. "To my shame I've overstepped my bounds twice now. You're a very attractive woman, but that's no excuse for my behavior every time I get within touching distance of you. I swear that as long as you're in my employ, you have nothing more to fear from me."

His words filled her with pain, but relief, too, because it meant no permanent damage had been done. She eyed him directly. "I was a willing participant, so it's obvious I haven't exactly been afraid of you, Nick."

"Nevertheless is there the possibility that you would forgive me and we could start over? Whatever else went on with me earlier has nothing to do with you. The thought that you might decide to leave me and Jamie before time terrifies the living daylights out of me."

A small smile broke the corners of her mouth. "It terrifies me, too, because I need the money you're paying me."

One dark brow dipped. "Do you need it enough to come with me this evening? We'll be taking Jamie to a party."

She folded her arms. "Why do I get the feeling this isn't just any party?"

"My parents expect me to marry again and have a woman picked out to become the next Mrs. Nicholas Wainwright. Her name is Jennifer

Ridgeway. I haven't seen her since her teens, but be assured her pedigree forms part of the framework of the upper crust. She'll be at the Yacht Club with her parents."

"I can see you're planning an all-out revolt."

"Yes." Reese could swear she saw fire in his eyes. "The sight of my son with his unsuitable nanny will dash every hope on all sides and make a statement that nothing else could do. It will be my virtual abdication from the family."

Whoa.

She felt Nick's conviction to her bones and knew tonight would change the course of his life and Jamie's forever. More than anything she wanted to be along to watch history being made.

"What should I wear?"

The lines darkening his face vanished. She saw his chest rise and fall due to the strength of his emotions. "How about that yellow outfit with a white ribbon around your ponytail?"

"I can do that. What about you?"

"No pedigreed member of the Yacht Club shows up in anything but formal dress. I'll wear a tux."

"And Jamie?"

A smile hovered around his compelling mouth. "His navy outfit with the Snoopy and his white high-tops. He'll be the first baby who ever made it inside the doors. If you're ready for Miroff and Hooplan, I know you'll be able to handle this crowd."

Her eyes suddenly moistened without her volition. That crowd included his parents, the two people responsible for bringing him into the world. She knew deep down somewhere he loved them because they *were* his parents. They'd bestowed every gift on him, given him every opportunity. There'd only been one thing lacking. She kept swallowing, trying to get rid of the thickness closing up her throat.

"How soon do you want to leave?"

"As soon as you can get Jamie and yourself ready. We'll be flying out to Long Island in the helicopter."

"I've had my shower. All I have to do is change clothes, then I'll take care of the baby and load his diaper bag."

He held her gaze. "One thing before we leave."

Adrenaline caused her heart to pound hard. "What is it?"

"I couldn't help but see the name of the person who sent you the postcard. Who's Rich?"

"My study partner at Wharton."

Nick cocked his head. "Does he measure up to your brilliance?"

Since emailing Rich a little while ago, Reese decided she'd better tell him now. "His full name is Richard Bonner."

His brows knit together. "That sounds familiar."

"It's because he just received word from the dean that he's been chosen to do an internship at Sherborne and Wainwright this fall."

He gave her an incredulous stare. "For years my uncle Lew has been in charge of choosing the interns. If they're not bright enough for him, he won't take one."

"Then there you go. Rich is the original whiz kid. He's apoplectic with joy about being chosen to work for the top company in New York. In case you're wondering, he has no idea you're my employer and I have no intention of ever telling him. Just imagine how crazy that would have been if you'd been stuck with me for a second round."

"Crazy doesn't begin to describe it," he ground out.

Two hours later the helicopter started to make its landing. Nick turned to her. "Welcome to The Sea Nook Yacht Club, listed on New York's Historical Register. Former home to the tall ships on Long Island's Gold Coast. Members only."

As it set down, Reese found the sight of the sprawling Tudor/Elizabethan estate overlooking the ocean surreal. Sailboats and yachts with pennants fluttering dotted the marina and beyond. To her, the world Nick had inhabited all these years was just as fantastic in its own way as Middle Earth or the Land of Oz.

Jamie reached for her after they climbed out of the helicopter. She held him as they walked next to Nick, who carried the baby's carryall and diaper bag across the grounds to the entrance. He looked adorable in his little navy suit. One day he would grow up to be as fantastic-looking as his gorgeous father, whose appearance in a black tux blew her away.

Nick had told her he wanted to arrive before anyone else. He preferred that his parents make the entrance with the Ridgeways instead of the other way around. The sight of Nick already in-stalled with his nanny and child would set the ground rules in concrete for the future.

The club had its own concierge, a burly man complete with beard, dressed like a proper sea captain in a smashing blazer and slacks. He swept across the enormous foyer with a smile on his face. "Good evening, Mr. Wainwright."

"How are you, Max?"

"Very well indeed. It's been a long time since we last saw you here. May I take this opportunity to tell you how sorry I am about the loss of Mrs. Wainwright? It was a shock to everyone."

"Thank you."

"You're the first of your party to arrive. We've put you out in the conservatory. Your father wanted the best view and we were able to ac-commodate him."

"Thank you."

The man's gaze flicked to Reese. "On vacation are you, miss? I'm sorry, but only members of the Yacht Club are allowed inside. You're welcome to stroll about the grounds with your child, of course."

Nick's eyes caught hers for a moment. She saw a wicked gleam of amusement in their dark depths. He was enjoying this. "She's with me, Max. Ms. Chamberlain is my nanny and this is my son, Jamie. He's just out of the hospital and won't be separated from us yet."

Reese had to give the host points for his aplomb in an awkward situation he'd most likely never had to deal with before. She could hear him trying to decide how to handle this. He cleared his throat. "Of course. Go right on out."

"Thank you, Max."

Reese had to put up with unfriendly stares and lifted brows from the beautiful people decked out in formal attire. Nick appeared oblivious. He led her through some tall paneled doors to another section of the club, which had to have been someone's spectacular estate at one time.

They came to a private room with high pan-eled ceilings, all of it surrounded by floor-to-ceiling glass windows, a modern innovation. It was almost like being on the water. He pulled out a chair where he put Jamie's carryall, then fastened him in it.

Reese sat down next to the baby. "I believe if I were prone to it, I'd be seasick about now."

A heart-stopping smile broke the corner of his mouth. "It's been known to happen in this room."

"What's the history of this place?"

He took a rattle from the diaper bag and handed it to Jamie, who claimed it in a fist and put it directly in his mouth. They both laughed.

"My mother's ancestor, Martin Sherborne, was an English sea captain in the early 1600s who traded in all sorts of lucrative things that brought him wealth. When he bought up a lot of the land around Sea Nook and had this place built, the colonial governor of New York conferred the title of Lordship of Sherborne on him.

"Eventually his grandson donated this place to the Sea Nook Township and built Sherborne

House where my mother grew up. It's located about ten miles from here. The estate borders Wainwright Meadows, known for its horses, where my father was born."

"How did they amass their wealth?"

"His ancestry developed tools for steam engines. Their manufacture proliferated beyond anyone's expectations. For those who live here, Sea Nook is known as Little England."

The sommelier approached, wanting to know their preference of wine. Nick turned to her. "Nothing for me," she responded.

"We'll both wait," Nick told him.

Reese leaned over to kiss the baby. "Did you hear all that your daddy said, Jamie? You could have been its newest prince," she teased, but she shouldn't have said anything because she saw Nick's jaw harden.

"*Could have* is exactly right. Don't look now but my cousin Greg has just arrived. It appears he's alone. He and his wife live at our property in the Hamptons. They're having difficulties right now."

Add one more property to the growing list. "Are you close to him?"

"No, but he works in the office and so far we've managed to get along."

"That's something at least."

When Nick smiled like that, she couldn't breathe. "At least," he drawled. "I'm afraid I've overloaded you with too much information."

"Not at all. It's like attending an on-site live college course covering the aspects of upper-class society in Colonial America. I wouldn't have missed it for the world."

"Greg!" Nick stood up and shook his cousin's hand. He was dark like Nick, a little shorter and heavier. "This is Reese Chamberlain from Lincoln, Nebraska. Reese, this is Greg Wainwright, one of the vice presidents of the brokerage."

"How do you do, Greg." She extended her hand, which he shook. Nick's cousin couldn't take his eyes off her. Nick didn't blame him. Anyone seeing Reese with that oval face and high cheekbones would call her a classic beauty. In the candlelight her light blue eyes let off an iridescent glow.

"Come around and say hi to Jamie."

His cousin's gaze shifted to the baby, but he didn't move from his stance. He flashed Nick one of those looks that said he needed to speak to him in private. *Not this time.* Nick had an idea what it was all about. In fact he'd been anticipating it.

"Won't you sit down? Or are you waiting for Uncle Lew?"

Greg shifted his weight, a sign that he was losing patience. "I need to talk to you alone for a minute. I tried to reach you earlier."

"I'm aware of that. You can say anything you want in front of Reese."

"Father sent me in here to talk sense to you."

"What sense is that?"

"This is a special dinner party." His brows lifted. "Max has let everyone know the…three of you are here," he said in a quieter voice.

Good. "Let's call a spade a spade. This was planned so the widower could meet wife number two, but my life has changed since Erica's death, Greg. No one owns me."

His face closed up. "Then I'm afraid you'll be dining in here alone."

"My parents should have thought of that before they tried to maneuver me into something that would hurt the Ridgeways. The fact is, no one consulted me. I intend to enjoy my dinner with my son and Ms. Chamberlain. You can tell that to Uncle Lew in private. What he tells father is up to him."

Greg studied him through new eyes. "What's happened to you?" It was a genuine question, requiring a genuine answer.

"The truth? I became a father, but I discovered I want to be a dad. Ms. Chamberlain is teaching me how."

His cousin seemed to have trouble articulating before he nodded to Reese and walked out of the room.

"*Nick—*"

The tremor in her voice was one of the most satisfying sounds he'd ever heard.

"The swordfish here is excellent by the way. If I order it for you, I promise you won't be disappointed."

CHAPTER EIGHT

For five solid days starting the next Monday, Reese took Jamie with her every morning and afternoon to hunt for an unfurnished studio apartment near Miroff's located on Broadway and Seventh. She needed one close enough to walk to her job.

By midafternoon she finally found it six blocks away above a small bookstore with signs saying that it was going out of business. You had to enter the store and walk to the back where there was a circular staircase leading to the studio. Both were owned by the bank.

She couldn't allow herself to think about where she was living right now. Moving from Nick's thirty-million-dollar penthouse to the tiny hole-in-the-wall that had no AC would be like going from the proverbial sublime to the proverbial ridiculous.

In order to hold it, she arranged for a six-month sublease starting now, even though the two guys living there wouldn't move out until the end of August. She would buy a futon and use it for a bed. Reese wouldn't need anything else since she'd be slaving day and night at the brokerage. If she was careful, the salary Nick paid her would cover the rent through January.

The small stipend she received from Miroff's would have to be enough for her food and any other incidentals. But at least she'd taken care of her housing problem and could spend the next week studying for her exam coming up a week from today. With a sigh of relief she phoned Paul and asked him to drive her and Jamie to the park.

"This is more like it, huh." She gave him a bunch of kisses before carrying him over to the pond. "You like these sailboats?" In her mind's eye she could see the larger sleeker ones and yachts moored at Sea Nook. That night had marked another change in Nick. He seemed charged by a new energy.

Throwing off the yoke of his other self acted

as some kind of catharsis. Twice this week he'd come home early, pulled on a pair of jeans with a T-shirt and made dinner. He put Jamie in the swing to watch him and held long conversations with him. When everything was ready, he'd invite her to eat on the terrace with them.

He cooked steaks and potatoes both times, reminding her of her father, who was a meat and potatoes man, too.

"Oh—my phone's ringing. Let's find out who it is." She pulled out her cell, but didn't recognize the name on the caller ID. After a slight hesitation she clicked on.

"Hello?"

"Ms. Chamberlain? This is Albert."

"Hi, Albert!"

"Sorry to disturb, but you have a visitor and I knew you'd gone out. He says it's urgent that he sees you. His name is Jeremy Young."

Reese closed her eyes tightly. She didn't blame her ex-fiancé for coming all this way without telling her. If their situations were reversed and she couldn't let him go without trying one more time, she would do the same thing. Her dad had probably told him about the internship and he'd made up his mind to talk to her again in the hope she wouldn't take it.

But it was no use. Their romance wasn't meant to be. Her plans for the future were set. She was so close now.

And then of course there was Nick. Every living moment with him meant falling deeper and deeper in love. She wouldn't be with him much longer, but it didn't matter. He'd colored her life forever. Nick and Jamie had her heart. All of it.

"I'm leaving for the apartment right now. Would you mind letting him in the penthouse? He's flown all the way from Nebraska and will appreciate freshening up before I get there."

"I'll be happy to."

"Thank you."

She hung up. "Let's go home, Jamie. We've got company."

When she pushed the stroller into the apartment a short time later, Jeremy stepped in the foyer from the living room.

"Reese—"

His was a dear face. Familiar, yet she couldn't conjure any feeling for him. Six months ago she couldn't have imagined not flying into his arms.

"It's good to see you, Jeremy." He was an attractive six-foot blond with dark blue eyes. He wore jeans and a button-down shirt with the hems out, his usual style when he wasn't in a business suit. But the wide smile that had been his trademark was missing. She saw pain in his eyes.

"You're not angry I just showed up?" he asked with an edge.

"No. How could I be? I'm only sad that you spent your time and hard-earned money for nothing."

"That's a matter of opinion. I've had some time to think since your dad told me you got that internship. I'd like to talk to you about it."

"Of course. Come out on the terrace with me and Jamie." She pushed the stroller through the apartment.

The second she opened the sliding door and they walked out, he let go with a long, low whistle. She watched him walk over to look out on the city. "My hell… I know there are people in the world who live like this, but to see it all up close makes me think I'm hallucinating."

"I've done a lot of that myself." She put Jamie on the lounger and changed him. Jeremy returned as she was snapping his suit.

"He's a cute baby. How old is he?"

"Four months."

"How much longer will you be here?"

"Until the end of August. That's when I start at Miroff's."

"Reese," he whispered. "I'll move to New York and get a bank job. If you're determined to be a career woman, then so be it. I don't want to lose you."

She hugged Jamie to herself, needing a minute to comprehend what he was saying. Reese could only imagine what it had taken for him to come to her like this. She needed to be so careful, but whatever she said, he was going to be hurt.

Taking a fortifying breath, she faced him. "I'll always love you, Jeremy, but I've had months to think about everything, too. Your instinct is to be the provider and come home to a wife who takes care of you and your children. A lot of men are like that. It's a wonderful instinct.

"What's wrong is that you met a woman like me who needs intellectual stimulation beyond mothering. I'd like to believe that in time I can do both. If we did get back together again, I'm sure it wouldn't be long before you'd start resenting me and I'd get upset with you because I would know I wasn't making you happy. It just wouldn't work."

"You're different than before," he said on a burst of anger.

She pressed her lips together. "I've had to put you away. It wasn't easy."

"But the point is, you *have* let me go."

"Yes," she answered honestly. This tearing each other apart was exactly what she didn't want to happen. "Jamie needs his bottle. I have to get it from the kitchen." Jeremy followed her. She took it out of the fridge and warmed it in the microwave.

"Has the baby's father made moves on you already?"

"Jeremy—please let's not do this."

"That's what you say when you want to avoid the issue."

She took the bottle out of the microwave. "I think you'd better go."

"No wonder you don't want to work anything out. There's nothing to stop you from staying on here permanently. You live in a virtual palace with New York at your feet. The money he's paying you is probably more than I make in a year at the bank."

Reese held the baby in her arms and fed him, praying Jeremy would see the futility in this and leave.

"Anyone home?"

Nick's deep male voice preceded him into the kitchen. She was sure Albert would have told him Jeremy was up here. Nick had announced himself in order to warn her he was on his way in.

The look on Jeremy's face reminded her of the Hirsts' expressions when they'd walked in the kitchen and had come face-to-face with Reese. Nick was a breed apart from other men. His polish and sophistication couldn't be denied. Besides his compelling physical attributes, there was something else you felt just being in his presence.

"Nick Wainwright?" She tried to keep her voice steady. "This is Jeremy Young."

Always the urbane host, Nick extended his hand. "It's nice to meet you, Jeremy."

"Likewise, Mr. Wainwright. You have a cute son."

"Thanks. I think so, too. Please excuse me for interrupting. I came to find him so we could play for a while." His eyes darted Reese an enigmatic glance before he lifted Jamie out of her arms. The baby was still drinking his bottle. "We're going out to the terrace, aren't we, sport."

Quiet reigned after his tall, hard-muscled body left the kitchen. Jeremy's eyes narrowed on Reese's upturned features. "Well...*that* just answered every question."

"Jeremy—" she called after him, but he was out of the kitchen and the penthouse like a shot.

He'd given her no choice by showing up without having called her first. How she hated hurting him. But if meeting Nick convinced him Reese was involved with her employer, then it had to be a good thing. Otherwise Jeremy would go on hoping for something that could never happen.

She rubbed her arms, feeling at a totally loose end. She was too tired from walking so much to go out again, but if she stayed in, she knew she wouldn't be able to study. Nick needed his time with Jamie. That left TV. Maybe a good film was on.

In the end she didn't bother to turn it on. Instead she flopped across her bed in turmoil. Five more weeks to go, but Reese was in trouble. The ache for Nick was growing intolerable.

She flung herself over on her back. Somehow she would have to find a way to be around Nick every day and not let him know the kind of pain she was in.

An hour later hunger drove her to the kitchen where she found him making ham-and-cheese sandwiches. She felt his gaze scrutinize her. "Do you and Jeremy have plans later?"

She shook her head. "He'll probably be back in Lincoln by tomorrow."

"Did you know he was coming?"

"No. His arrival was a complete surprise. Albert called me while Jamie and I were at the park."

He pursed his lips. "Then let's eat. Grab us a couple of colas from the fridge and we'll go out on the terrace."

"That sounds good."

He reached for a bag of potato chips. Together they carried everything outside to the table. After they sat down, she opened her cola and drank almost half of it, not realizing how thirsty she was.

Nick relaxed in the chair, extending his long legs in front of him while he swallowed two sandwiches in succession. "Leah and I had a conversation the other day. When she chose you for the nanny, there were three other women who could have done the job. One of them is probably still available to work. But even if they've all found other employment, there'll be someone else."

A sharp, stabbing pain almost incapacitated her. "Why are you telling me this?"

"Because you need to be free to work things out with Jeremy. The man didn't fly all this way unless he were still terribly in love with you. I saw the look on his face. He couldn't say what he had to say with me walking in on him. If you go home now, it's possible you'll straighten out your differences and end up getting married."

Nick's last stab had dissected her heart. "You mean the way you and Erica straightened out yours?" Her pain had to find an outlet. He might just as well have been her patronizing uncle Chet patting her on the head and telling her she was too pretty to study so much. The guys would be intimidated.

He stopped eating and sat forward. "I was never in love with her."

The bald revelation was swallowed up in her pain because he wasn't in love with Reese, either. Not even close or he couldn't have suggested she abandon Jamie and follow Jeremy home.

In a rare display of sarcasm she said, "Well, that's an excellent explanation for why your marriage fell apart. Jeremy and I have irreconcilable problems *now,* and would never make it to the altar."

"Love is a rare thing," he came back in a mild mannered voice, the kind that set her teeth on edge. "You had that going for you once. He hasn't given up. It appears to me that anything's still possible."

"Not when he doesn't want a working wife."

"Would it be so terrible if you compromised in order for the two of you to be together?"

"Terrible?" she cried. "It would be disastrous."

"Why?"

"Because then neither of us would be happy." She shook her head. "You really don't understand. Let me ask you something. After you'd studied all those years to make your place at Wainwright's, what if Erica had said, 'You don't need to go to work now, Nick. Stay home with me. I have enough money to take care of both of us for a lifetime.'"

His lids drooped so the black lashes shuttered his eyes. "You can't use me or Erica for an example."

The first sparks of temper shot through her. "Why not? Blue bloods still make up part of our world, albeit a tiny percentage of the population."

She watched him squeeze his cola can till it dented. "Because for one thing, the kind of love that should bind a man and woman didn't define our relationship."

"Supposing it had?"

Nick didn't like being put on the spot. It only made her more determined to get her point across.

"What if you'd both been crazy about each other and she'd told you she wanted you to be home with her and the baby. Several babies maybe. What would you have said?"

His hand absently rubbed his chest. "It's an absurd question, Reese."

"Of course it's absurd to *you*. You're a man, right? And in the world you've come from, a man is better than a woman." She jumped to her feet, unable to keep still.

A white ring of anger had encircled his lips, but she couldn't stop now. "It would be purgatory for you if you couldn't get up every morning of life eager to match wits against your competitors.

"I heard your whole genealogy the other night at the Yacht Club. You come from an ancestry that made things happen. Like them you live to pull off another million deal today, and another one tomorrow, and all the tomorrows after that. It's what makes you, *you*."

He pushed himself away from the table and stood up. "And you're telling me you feel the exact same way?"

She let out a caustic laugh. "That's inconceivable to you, isn't it. *Moi?* A mere woman who has that same fire in her? Impossible. A woman who wants to make a difference? Unheard of, right?"

"Frankly, yes," he said in a voice of irony, "particularly when I see the way you are with Jamie. No one would ever guess you weren't his mother."

"You're not even listening to me because in your eyes a woman can't be both." She circled in front of him. "Let me tell you something about yourself, Nick. Though you've come a long way to rid yourself of the shackles imposed by thirty-four years of emotional neglect, you'll never be a man who could compromise on something so vital to your very existence as your work."

The glitter in those black depths should have warned her, but she was just getting warmed up.

"Yet you hand out advice to me and suggest I go home to patch things up with Jeremy as if my problem is nothing more than a bagatelle that can be swept under the rug. Be a good girl and do what girls are supposed to do, Reese. Let Jeremy take care of business so you can take care of his babies. Compromise for the sake of your love. That's great advice, Mr. Wainwright, as long as *you're* not the one being forced to do the compromising."

"Are you finished?" he asked as if he'd grown tired of her tantrum. She couldn't bear his condescension.

"Not quite," she fired back. "One day I intend to open my own brokerage company right here in New York and be a *huge* success. In the meantime I'm contracted with you to take care of Jamie until I start my internship at Miroff's. For your information I never renege on my commitments, unlike you who would send me back to Nebraska on the next flight without a qualm."

She paused at the sliding door. "If you need me, I'll be in my bedroom studying."

Nick buzzed his secretary. "Leah? I'll be in Lew's office for a while." He'd done a little research and had requested this conference. "Hold my calls." If Reese needed him, she'd phone his cell. But she didn't need or want anything from him.

He still had the scars from their scalding conversation of three weeks ago. Nothing about their routine had altered since then, but the atmosphere had undergone a drastic change. When they talked about Jamie, everything was civil, but the gloom that had enveloped him after Erica had died couldn't compare to the darkness enveloping him now. A wall of ice had grown around his nanny. He couldn't find her anywhere. Her love and animation were reserved exclusively for his son.

Unable to take it, he'd gone off to Martha's Vineyard with Jamie every Friday afternoon. They'd sailed the whole weekend. Sunday nights he returned to the penthouse, always finding her bedroom door closed. He'd see the light beneath and know she was in there.

Today he knew she was taking her online exam. When he'd told her he would stay home to keep Jamie occupied, she'd told him it wouldn't be necessary. She'd handle both just fine, underscoring her assertions made during their heated exchange earlier.

On that black night Reese had delivered some salvos he'd never seen coming. Stunned by their impact, he'd barely functioned since then. This morning he'd found himself floundering in a dark sea and knew he couldn't go this way any longer.

The emotional temperature was distinctly cooler in his uncle's office. Lew sat at his desk, more or less squinting up at Nick as he walked in. Nick had committed the unpardonable at the club for which he'd been collectively shunned by the family.

That didn't bother him, but it had thrown Lew out of his comfort zone. The business Nick was about to conduct with him would dissolve what little relationship they had left. This meeting would supply the final punctuation mark.

"What was so important I had to tell my secretary to cancel my last two appointments for the day?"

Nick sat on the arm of one of the leather love seats. "I'm resigning from the company effective immediately and wanted you to be the first to know, besides Leah, of course."

"What?" Suddenly the mask of implacability fell from his face to reveal a vulnerability Nick had never seen before. "You haven't told Stan? Not even your father?"

"No. I'll leave that to you since you're closest to them."

"But you *can't* resign—this place would fall around our ears without you."

A genuine emotion for once. Who would have believed?

"I've named Greg as my replacement in the resignation letter I gave to Leah this morning. It's been dated and notarized. Your son has earned the right to head the firm. I've earned the right to do what's best for me."

He shook his head, clearly aghast. "What are your plans?"

"I'm keeping those to myself for the time being. This is my last day here. Except for a few personal items I'm taking with me, my office is ready for Greg to claim. My accounts are now his. Leah will stay on as his private secretary to make certain there's a smooth transition."

His uncle rose slowly to his feet. "Are you dying of a fatal disease?"

Nick made a sound in his throat. Illness was the only reason Lew could possibly imagine for one of the family to do something unprecedented and heretical.

"In a manner of speaking, but that's confidential. I'll be seeing you." He got up from the chair to shake his hand. His uncle's response reminded him of a person who'd just gone into shock.

On Nick's way out he stopped by Leah's office. "Is everything done?"

"It is."

"Did you get everything I needed?"

"It's all there in your briefcase. Paul's waiting out in front."

"You're the best friend a man ever had." The fact that it was a woman didn't escape him.

He slipped her an envelope with a check in it made out to her, gave her a hug, then rode down the elevator and walked out of the building as if he had wings on his feet. A few minutes later he walked in the door of the penthouse feeling as if he'd been given his get-out-of-jail-free card.

"Reese?"

When she didn't answer, he headed for the terrace. The second he opened the sliding door he could hear her laughter. Over the hedge he could see her and Jamie in the pool. She'd pinned her ponytail on top of her head and was pulling him around on an inflated plastic duck. Evidently her exam was over and she'd decided to let off some excess energy. She was a knockout in that tangerine-colored bikini.

Since Reese hadn't seen him yet, he dashed back to his bedroom and changed into his swimming trunks. On his way out he grabbed a couple of bath towels and headed for the pool once more.

To his delight she and Jamie were still moving around in the water. She sprinkled his tummy several times, provoking little laughs from him. Would the day might come when she'd do that to Nick, but it would be more than laughter she'd get in return.

He dived in the deep end and swam underwater on purpose where he could feast his eyes on her long, gorgeous legs. They were an enticement he couldn't resist, but he *had* to.

A few feet from her, he surfaced and heaved himself up on the tile. She was all eyes when he came out of the water. *"Nick—"*

Yes, Nick. For a split second he could have sworn he saw longing in them before she turned to Jamie, who'd become her shield. "How was the exam?" His eyes were drawn to the small nerve throbbing at the base of her throat.

"Maybe I had a different battery than others who've taken it, but it wasn't as hard as I'd thought it would be."

"I'm sure you're glad it's over."

"Definitely." She twirled the duck around so Jamie could see him. "He's been waiting for you to come home."

What a sight! Her blue eyes were more dazzling

than the water. He slid back in the pool and swam over to his son.

"Look at you having the time of your life out here." Jamie almost fell out of the floater trying to get to him. With a laugh, Nick caught him up to his shoulder and kissed him. While he was enjoying his son, Reese did a backflip and swam to the other end of the pool to get out. It was a good exit line, but he wasn't about to let her get away with it.

"Reese?" She looked back at him as she was about to walk off. "Whatever your plans are this evening, I need to talk to you first. Give me ten minutes and I'll meet you in the dining room."

"All right."

When she'd gone, he looked down at Jamie. "We've got to get out and dressed, sport. Tonight's kind of important." He swam over to the steps and climbed out. After wrapping him in a towel, he headed for the nursery and put him in a diaper and shirt.

Since he seemed content, Nick let him stay in the crib with his pacifier. Then he went to his bedroom to shower and change into trousers and a sport shirt.

Fifteen minutes later he gathered Jamie and the swing. Reese was already waiting for them at the table in the dining room with her ponytail redone. The waiter had already brought their meal and had set everything up.

With Jamie ensconced in the swing, Nick was able to concentrate on Reese, who'd changed into a pale blue cotton top and denims. "Do you like lamb?" He lifted the covers off their plates.

"I love it."

"Then I think you'll enjoy Cesar's rack of lamb." So saying, he poured both of them water before starting to eat.

She followed suit. "Sounds like you're celebrating."

"I thought it sounded like a good idea. Your exam is over, and a Greek friend of mine named Andreas Simonides has invited me to spend some time with him and his wife, Gabi, on the island of Milos in the Aegean. We met a few years ago when we were both single and did some sailing together. He has stayed here at the penthouse on several occasions. He's married now with a three-month-old baby girl himself and is anxious to meet Jamie. So I told him I'd come."

"That sounds exciting." She was doing her best to act pleased for him, but she'd been with him and Jamie every day for weeks now. The thought of a separation caused such a great upheaval inside her, she could hardly breathe from the pain.

"I think so, too."

"When are you leaving?"

"Tomorrow morning."

That soon? "How long will you be gone?" She fought to keep her voice steady.

"Two weeks."

She didn't have time to hide her shock.

"Now that I've got Jamie, I feel like a long holiday. You'll be coming with us of course. His wife is an American, which will be nice for you."

Reese and Gabi sat in deck chairs on the patio surrounding the pool of the Simonides villa, watching the babies in their swings. Little Cristiana was as golden-blonde as Jamie was dark headed.

They looked adorable together. Reese had never envied anyone until now, but she envied Gabi, who had Andreas's love and his baby.

Moaning inwardly, she looked all around her. The Simonides' family retreat was so gorgeous, it was beyond impossible to describe. A myriad of white, cubed-styled villas were clustered against the cliff abounding in flowers of every color and greenery all the way down to the water. There the white sand merged with an aquamarine ocean that took your breath.

This morning the men had gone fishing early, but they'd promised to be back by lunchtime. Reese's holiday would have been heaven on earth if she and Nick were lovers, but such wasn't the case. Nick had behaved like the perfect employer, albeit a kind, generous one. But he'd kept his distance and had given her plenty of time off so she could enjoy herself without having to tend Jamie every second.

Gabi was a sweetheart. She'd been the manager of an advertising agency back in Alexandria, Virginia, so they had a lot in common. The two of them had taken to each other at once and had flown to Athens several times to meet other members of the Simonides clan. They shopped and went to the opera, but for the most part, the time was spent on Andreas's fabulous gleaming white luxury cabin cruiser probably forty to forty-five feet long.

With the babies, the four of them visited all the wonders of the island. They walked through the little villages, ate local food, swam at the unique beaches and soaked up the Grecian sun in absolute luxury. But this idyllic time was fast coming to a close. Tomorrow they were due to fly back to New York.

True to their word, Nick came out on the patio with Andreas, both in shorts and nothing else, just as lunch was about to be served. The latter kissed his wife soundly before pulling Cristiana out of her swing to kiss her.

Writhing with unassuaged longings, Reese got up and slipped on her beach jacket while Nick grabbed Jamie and got into the pool with him. When they emerged and everyone was seated around the patio table eating, Nick glanced at her. "I've made arrangements for one of the maids to tend Jamie this afternoon so I can take you to a beach you haven't seen before."

"It's our favorite spot on Milos," Andreas said, covering his wife's hand.

"That sounds wonderful," Reese murmured, though something inside told her she'd be a fool to spend that much time alone with Nick. But she didn't want to argue in front of their hosts who'd been so fabulous to them, she'd never be able to repay them.

"Good. You're already in your bathing suit, so as soon as you've finished eating, we'll go."

Reese swallowed the last of her iced lemon drink and got up to give Jamie a goodbye kiss. "Be a good boy. We'll be back soon." The baby got all excited. His reaction warmed her heart.

"We'll go down this path." He started ahead of her. They zigzagged down to the private pier lined on both sides with various types of boats. Nick headed for a small jet boat they hadn't ridden in yet.

When he helped her to climb in, she felt fire shoot up her arm. This really wasn't a good idea, but she'd said she would go. Somehow she needed to turn off the hormones. To her chagrin she didn't know how.

Nick was so at home on the water, you would have thought he lived here year-round. After handing her a life jacket and telling her to put it on, he untied the ropes and they backed out into the blue bay. Once they got beyond the buoys, they sped through the glasslike water of the Aegean. Glorious.

When he turned his head and smiled at her, she was in such a euphoric state, she felt as if they were flying. "There's no beach in the world like the one you're going to see."

"I can't imagine anything more beautiful than the ones we've been to already."

"Papafragas is different. Have you had a good time so far? Feel like you've gotten away from all your studies and worries?"

Her lips curved into a full-bodied smile. "A good time?" she mocked. "That's like asking me if I've been having a good time in paradise."

"There are levels of excitement, even in paradise."

She averted her eyes. Yes. To be loved and

make love with Nick would be the pinnacle, the only part of paradise she would never know.

They eventually drew close to another part of the island. Nick cut the motor and the momentum drove them toward a cave opening.

"I feel like a pirate."

He flashed her a penetrating glance. "Andreas tells me they used to roam these waters. We'll swim from here." Nick got out of his seat and lowered the anchor. "If you get tired, you've got your life jacket on to support you and I'll take us the rest of the way."

At the thought of him touching her one more time, adrenaline shot through her system, driving her to her feet. Without waiting for Nick, she leaped off the side and headed through the cave opening. Once beyond it she realized it was a long, natural, fjordlike swimming pool surrounded by walls of white rock.

"This is fantastic!"

"This is fantastic!" came the echo. She laughed in delight.

He caught up to her and they did the side stroke as they headed for the other end. His dark eyes held hers. "There are half a dozen caves in here. If we had more time, we could explore them."

Time. Her enemy.

Another fifty yards lay a strip of warm white sand from the sun finding its way down between the walls of rock. Nick reached it first and pulled her onto the sand. They both turned over to lie on their backs.

"You were right, Nick. This beach is incredible."

"Andreas said he used to come here with his brother Leon to play space aliens."

Her laughter rang out over and over because of the echo. "I love it here!" she cried. Again, her words reverberated, *Love it here, love it here, love it here.*

"You sound happy, Reese."

"Not happy. Something so much more, but there is no word in English for what I'm feeling right now."

"Then you admit you needed a vacation, too."

She let out an exasperated sound. "You know I did. I've been in school for so long, I almost forgot what it's like to play. Of course there's playing, and then there's the Wainwright-Simonides way of having fun."

This time Nick's deep, rich laughter resounded against the walls.

Reese smiled at him. "You sound like King Poseidon in here, coming up from the sea for a breather because he's happy, too."

"I am. When I think of the dark place I was before I hired you, I can't relate to it anymore. I have you to thank for that. There's no way in this world I'll be able to repay you for showing me how to be a dad to my son."

Her eyes filled with tears she fought to hold back. "You just have by giving me this trip. Andreas and Gabi are the nicest people I've ever known. It's been an experience I'll cherish all my life."

"I'm glad then," he said in a husky voice. Quick as lightning he rolled on his side, bringing him close to her. "Reese—" He put his hand on her arm, but she wasn't destined to succumb to her needs because four people had started down the rocks from the surface on their end of the beach and their voices were already making echoes.

She heard a groan of protest come out of Nick before he got up and pulled her to her feet. His eyes fused with hers. "A serpent has entered Eden. Let's go."

Much as she hated the intrusion, those swimmers had probably prevented her from confessing all to Nick and begging him to make love to her. She'd passed up her chance when they'd gone sailing at Martha's Vineyard. This time she wouldn't have had the willpower to deny herself or him anything.

Other swimmers were pouring in at the other end of the cave entrance. Apparently it was a very popular place in the late afternoon. She and Nick had been lucky to have it to themselves for as long as they did.

On the other side of the rocks were two more boats with even more people jumping off to enter the cave. They asked questions of Nick in Greek. It gave her time to hurry around the end of their jet boat and climb the ladder before he could touch her. The unforgettable memories were storing up like mad.

During the trip back, Nick was unusually quiet. She was glad, because she was in no frame of mind to make small talk. It was good they were leaving in the morning. She couldn't take any more of this kind of togetherness, knowing it had no future.

As soon as they pulled up to the pier, she told him she was anxious to shower. After that she would relieve the maid of taking care of Jamie and would see him at dinner.

It turned out to be a big family affair with many of Andreas's family in attendance. So many children. So much love. All of them belonged to each other except for her and Nick.

Reese was actually glad when morning came and the three of them left in the helicopter for Athens. Once they were back in New York, they would return to their normal routine. Nick would go to work and Reese would continue to love the baby and take him everywhere with her until…

She couldn't think about *until*. The thought of moving to that tiny little room and starting her internship without them was anathema to her.

CHAPTER NINE

REESE had endured a terrible last night on Milos. She'd finally fallen asleep on a wet pillow. By the time they were in flight on Nick's private jet and she'd given Jamie a bottle, she was so tired, Nick took the baby from her and told her to go to sleep.

She didn't waken until the fasten-seat-belts sign flashed on. Jamie was strapped in his carrycot in the other club seat sound asleep. Reese looked at Nick.

"I'm sorry I slept so long."

"Evidently you needed it." He was staring at her rather strangely. She didn't understand.

"Is there something wrong?"

"Not at all."

Maybe it was her imagination. After leaving Greece, it was probably hard for him to come back to the penthouse, which was a huge reminder of the sadness he'd lived through during the past year.

The jet touched down and taxied to a stop in front of the private hangar. Out the window she saw Paul leave the limo and walk toward them. With Nick, everything ran like clockwork.

She undid her seat belt and stood up to stretch. Paul came on board and nodded to her before carrying Jamie off the jet. When she turned to Nick, he smiled. "You look rested."

"I am. How did Jamie do during the flight?"

"He was perfect."

"That's good." Why was he standing there, looking at her in such an odd way again?

"It's because of the expert care you've given him. He's thriving because of you. Now it's time for you to have a few weeks to yourself before you start your internship at Miroff's. My pilot has instructions to fly you to Lincoln as soon as I get off."

What? Her world started to reel.

"Andreas and I talked about it and thought it best that both you and Jamie have a clean break from each other. He's had maids and a housekeeper fussing over him while we were in Greece. Hopefully he'll adjust to the new nanny Leah has found for me. Since I don't have one complaint about you, I'm going to trust her judgment again."

He was sending her back to Nebraska, just like that?

"Please accept my gratitude for all you've done by accepting this last gift. As your employer, I have the right." So saying, he reached in his pocket for an envelope and handed it to her. "Inside this is an airline ticket for your flight when you come back to New York in two weeks."

Her mouth had gone dry to the point it was impossible to swallow. "I couldn't take it."

"If that's your decision, but I wish you'd reconsider." He took it and tossed it on the seat of the club car next to her. "The return date has been left open in case you didn't plan to arrive until the day you start at Miroff's. Since I put your full salary for the three months specified into your account the day you came to work for me, I don't think I've left anything out."

No. Nothing. Absolutely nothing.

"I instructed Rita to pack the rest of your belongings. Paul brought them to the airport. They're being put on board right now. Since I'm sure your parents would want to know you're coming, why not phone them before the pilot's ready to take off?"

"I'll do that," she answered numbly.

"If you need anything, just ask the steward."

"I will. Give Jamie a goodbye kiss for me."

"Of course." He studied her for a moment longer. "Miroff's is going to be lucky to get you. Have a safe flight."

"I can't face the family tonight, Mom. Yesterday when I got home, I thought I could." Reese had been shucking the corn while her mom finished fixing the green salad for the barbecue. Her dad was outside getting the grill warmed up. The whole family would descend en masse in a little while.

"I know you're absolutely devastated, but that's the very reason why you need to."

Tears gushed down her tanned face. "You'll never know the pain I'm in. I honestly thought

Nick had fallen in love with me, too. I'm such a little fool I can't believe it."

Her mom flashed her a commiserating look. "You know what you're going to have to do?" She sliced two rows of tomatoes and onions in perfect sections. "Put this experience behind you. I realize that's easy for me to say, but in a way he's done you a great favor. Another two weeks of togetherness would have made the parting nearly impossible. You have to think of Jamie."

"You're right." She wiped her wet cheeks with the back of her hands. "Nick could see how attached I've become to him. I love that little boy. He's so cute and darling, you have no idea."

"I'm sure he loves *you*. The hospital visit bonded you."

"I know," she said in a haunted whisper.

"Thanks to Nick's generosity, we have two weeks to talk this over without you having money worries or deadlines."

At any other time in her life Reese might have echoed her mom's feelings, but it was agony being away from Nick. Every time she thought about him and Jamie, she got this pain in her chest and could hardly breathe.

"Do you have pictures of them?"

"Yes. I had doubles made up for his baby book and kept some for me. I'll get them." She dashed through the house to her bedroom and grabbed the packet off her dresser. "These are the ones I took of them the day we put the nursery together. And here are some I took while we were on Milos."

Her mom wiped her hands and studied them. When she lifted her head, she took a long time before she spoke because her lovely gray-blue eyes said it all. "I think your pain is going to take a long time to go away. It's a good thing you'll be working so hard at Miroff's."

Her mom was right. She needed family around. Her sister Carrie would be here soon with her two children. The distraction would help, but then everyone would go home after the weekend was over and Reese would once more be a prisoner to her memories.

She didn't know how she was she going to make it through tonight, let alone the rest of her life without him and Jamie. But to her shock, she was still alive the next day and the day after that. Her dad put her to work at the lumberyard, which saved her life. She answered phones and did odd jobs for him.

On Friday of the second week her mom phoned the office. "I'm glad you answered it. An express-mail envelope just came for you. I had to sign for it." Reese's heart began to thud. Intellectually she knew it wasn't from Nick, but her heart was crying out otherwise. "Do you want me to open it?"

"Please. It could be my exam results, but I thought they'd just send my score online."

"Well, you *are* their top student."

Reese smiled to herself in spite of her pain. "I'm the luckiest girl in the world to have a cheering section like you, Mom. What's in it?"

"A letter from Miroff and Hooplan." Reese had been waiting for final instructions from them, but her disappointment was so acute that it wasn't from Nick, she sank down in the chair. "Do you want me to read it?"

"Yes. I need to know when to make my return flight."

"Let's see. It's very short. 'Dear Ms. Chamberlain, congratulations on your new appointment. Please report to our office on Monday, August 29, at 9:00 a.m. for an orientation that will last until 4:00 p.m.'"

"That's two days sooner than my studio apartment will be vacant—"

"Don't worry. Your father and I want to pay for a decent hotel for you to stay in until you're settled."

"You're wonderful. Thanks, Mom."

"It says, 'We look forward to working with you. Sincerest Regards, Gerald Soffe, Vice President of Internal Affairs.' Well, honey, that makes it official."

The taxi dropped Reese off in front of Miroff's on Broadway. She'd decided to dress in a summer two-piece suit in a melon color. Maybe she could get away with a ponytail later on, but today she wore her hair down. It fell from a side part and had a tendency to curl in the humidity.

She paid the driver and went inside carrying her briefcase that held her laptop. "I'm Reese Chamberlain. I was told to report to Mr. Soffe," she told the receptionist.

"Second door down the hall on your left. He's expecting you."

"Thank you." She started for her destination, realizing she didn't feel the excitement she should have. For the past two weeks she'd been in a depressed state. Coming back to New York had made it worse.

When she spotted his name and title on the door, she opened it and walked in to find another receptionist, who lifted her red head. "You must be Ms. Chamberlain."

"Yes."

"Go right on in."

"Thank you."

The second she entered the man's office, she saw a familiar figure seated behind the desk and let out a cry.

It was Nick!

He'd kept his dark tan since their return from Greece and his black hair had grown longer. In a dove-gray summer suit with a darker gray shirt and no tie, he was gorgeous beyond belief.

"Hello, Reese." His eyes played over her slowly, missing nothing from her head to her low heels. "Come all the way in and sit down."

He didn't need to tell her that. By the time she reached the nearest chair, she was out of breath and her legs no longer supported her. "H-how's Jamie?" she stammered like a fool.

"Other than missing you, he's perfect."

She'd started trembling and couldn't stop. "What's going on? Where's Mr. Soffe?"

"He's a professional friend of mine. I asked him to make himself scarce while I talked to you first."

Maybe she was hallucinating. "Why would you do that?"

"When my uncle Lew assigned Rich Bonner to be the fall intern, he made a mistake. You were the top candidate from Wharton's, but as you know, blue bloods don't consider women equal to men, so he chose Mr. Bonner, who'd been ranked second highest in his class."

Reese wanted to die. "You'll never forgive me

for that, will you. Don't you know how sorry I am?" she cried out emotionally.

His eyes flashed dark fire. "You have nothing to feel guilty about. Why would you when it was the truth! I straightened things out with Gerald. He's been in contact with Mr. Bonner, who will be coming to work for Miroff's in a few days."

With those words, Reese felt as if she was in a strange dream where nothing was as it should be. "Don't think I don't appreciate what you've tried to do for me, Nick, but I don't want anything changed, because I have no intention of working for your corporation. Even though I was a woman, Miroff's took me on. I plan to make them very happy with their choice."

He studied her for a tension-filled moment. "In that case you'll have to walk across the street with me while we visit with Greg, Uncle Lew's son. You met him the night we had dinner at the Yacht Club. You need to tell him what you just told me. Then he'll make it right with Gerald and your friend Rich."

Searing pain drove through her to think that

in the future she'd be working across the street from Nick. She couldn't bear it.

He came around the desk and picked up her briefcase. "Shall we go?"

How many times had she heard him say that before in connection with Jamie. Like déjà vu she left the building with him. Whenever they walked together, she had to hurry to keep up with his long strides. They maneuvered the crowded crosswalk and eventually entered the tall doors of his family's firm.

Nick nodded to the foyer receptionist and continued to the elevator. "Greg's in his office waiting for us." They emerged on the third floor and entered a door marked Gregory Wainwright, President.

President? But *Nick* was the CEO.

Before she could ask what it meant, Leah Tribe was there to greet her. "We meet again, Ms. Chamberlain."

But Mrs. Tribe was *Nick's* secretary. What was going on? "How are you, Mrs. Tribe?"

"I couldn't be better. I hear you're going to be working for us. How do you feel about that?"

How did she feel? "I'm afraid there's been a mistake. I need to talk to Mr. Wainwright."

"Oh—" The secretary looked surprised. "Go right on in. He's expecting you."

Nick slanted her a glance she couldn't read. Still carrying her briefcase, he led her inside the inner door.

Reese remembered Nick's cousin, who got to his feet. He was a man in his thirties who bore a slight resemblance to Nick, though he was shorter and less fit looking.

"Greg? You were introduced to Ms. Chamberlain before. Apparently there's been a mistake. She intends to stay with Miroff's and you'll be getting Mr. Bonner as planned."

His cousin looked completely thrown, but before he could say anything there was a buzz, then Leah Tribe's voice came over the intercom. "I'm sorry to bother you, Mr. Wainwright, but Stan needs a minute of your time for something that can't wait."

"I'll be right there, Leah. Nick?" He turned to him. "If you'll keep Ms. Chamberlain occupied, I'll be back as soon as I can."

The door shut, enclosing the two of them in a silence so quiet, she was sure Nick could hear her heart hammering. He took his seat behind the desk. She found a wing chair opposite him and sat down.

"Did they let you go because of what happened at the Yacht Club?"

"No. It was my choice. In fact I stepped down before I left for Greece with you and Jamie."

"Why?" she asked in shock. "I don't understand."

He stared at her for a long time. "Because I wanted to be free. You see…I'm getting married right away. You could say I'm starting a new life."

Reese thought she would faint, but she wouldn't let him know how his news had affected her. "Someone you've known for a long time?"

Nick cocked his head. "Do you remember the day you stepped into my limo for the first time?"

She frowned. "Surely you don't need an answer to that question."

"Surely you shouldn't have had to ask me that

question at all," he fired back. "Who else would I marry but *you*."

Blood hammered in her ears. "Be serious, Nick," her voice trembled.

"I would never be anything else *but* with the woman who's about to become my wife and Jamie's legal mother. We took a vote while we were on Milos and decided it was you or no one. Andreas and Gabi seconded the motion."

Reese shook her head. "I'm so confused I must have missed something. I'm going to work at Miroff's. How could you think I would be your wife?"

"It's possible to be both. You convinced me of that a month ago during one of our more scintillating conversations. Here's my proposal. We get married in Nebraska and honeymoon there. I want to meet your family. Then we'll come back to the penthouse and you start work. I'll be a stay-at-home daddy during your internship."

She couldn't possibly be hearing him correctly.

"When you're through at Miroff's and graduate, we'll take care of Jamie together while you decide where and how you're going to start your own brokerage firm. You'll be doing it all on your own. When you're ready to take on a partner, I'm your man behind the scenes."

"Nick—"

"We'll get my office set up in the other bedroom at the end of the hall like you wanted to do in the first place. I'll work for you at home. I'm counting on you being a huge success because you're going to be the one bringing in the money for both of us, starting with the stipend you'll make being an intern. You see, I've signed away my entire inheritance to the family."

Her gasp reverberated in the room.

"The money I earned myself allowed me to buy the penthouse. But it represents my old life with Erica. When your company gets off the ground, I want to sell it and buy us a house outside the city. Somewhere in a residential neighborhood where Jamie and another brother or sister can play with other children on the block and have a dog. The rest I'll invest for our children's future."

"Oh, darling—"

Reese flew out of the chair and around the

desk. Her feet never touched the ground before she landed in his arms. She threw them around his neck, so deliriously happy she couldn't talk. Instead she started sobbing. "Nick— I love you and Jamie so terribly. You just don't know—"

"Tell me about it," he whispered into her hair, crushing her to death.

Neither of them was aware Mrs. Tribe had come in until they heard her voice. "I like what I see, you two. I like it very much."

Nick lifted his mouth from Reese's. "Thank heaven for you, Leah."

When the door closed, Reese urgently pressed her mouth to his again. She couldn't get enough and never would, but her euphoria was interrupted once more. This time she heard a baby crying, but it had lost its newborn sound.

"Jamie?"

"Who else? He's living for you to hug and kiss him, but this is one time he's going to have to get in line."

Miroff's closed down for Christmas on the eighteenth, which would be Reese's last working day as an intern. But when she approached Gerald a few days before and told him she had a special surprise for Nick that required the last day off, her boss was happy to give it to her.

In fact he handed her an enormous bonus for her outstanding work. Then he offered her a job with his company. She hadn't expected either offering and was overwhelmed.

After expressing her gratitude, she told him she couldn't accept the offer because she and Nick had other plans. But she thanked him with a big hug, which he reciprocated, and she gave him his Christmas present. It was a box of chocolate truffles from his favorite candy shop. She'd given the same gift to Leah.

On the seventeenth, she kissed her husband and son goodbye and pretended to leave for work. Paul was waiting for her out in front of the apartment building as always. When she climbed in the limo, she asked him to drive her to the studio apartment she'd leased in August. Unbeknownst to Nick, Paul had been bringing her here most every working day on her lunch break for the past four months.

When she got out of the limo into the freezing cold, she walked up to the window. He put it down. "This is for you. Merry Christmas." She handed him the gift she'd had engraved for him. It was a gold ring with a stunning black onyx stone. Inside it read, Ever Faithful.

"I don't know what Nick and I would do without you." She smiled. "Until later."

He winked. "I can't wait to see Nick's face when I pull up with him."

"I'm living for that, too."

When he drove off, she walked toward the entrance of the former bookshop with so much excitement, she could scarcely contain it. A large, classy-looking black-and-white-striped awning gave the storefront a whole new look and caught the eye of every passerby. Her eyes traced the formal gold lettering on the squeaky-clean glass door with a stunning holly wreath hanging above.

Chamberlain & Wainwright Brokerage.

For the rest of the day she wrapped presents and put them under the lighted Christmas tree in the center of the room. By two o'clock everything was ready upstairs and down.

With her pulse racing, she reached for her cell and phoned Nick.

"Reese?" She hadn't heard that tinge of anxiety in his voice for a long time.

"Hi, darling."

"Is anything wrong? You don't usually call me this time of day."

"Everything's fine. I'm just tired and feel like leaving early. Gerald gave me the time off. I thought if you and Jamie came and picked me up, we could have an early dinner at a cozy little place I've found."

Whenever Nick worried, he was always quiet before he responded. "We'll come right now. Are you sure you're all right? You've been working so hard you've knocked yourself out."

"No harder than you. How's our boy?"

"He's been trying to stand up, but keeps falling down."

"I have no doubts he'll be walking sooner than most children his age. Come soon? I miss you both horribly."

Convinced something was wrong, Nick phoned Paul and told him to bring the car out front. Getting up from his office chair, he rushed down the hall to the nursery. Jamie wasn't due to wake up from his afternoon nap for another half hour, but it couldn't be helped. It wasn't like Reese to call in the afternoon. That's when she was normally in conference with the staff.

"Sorry, sport." Jamie was still half-asleep while Nick changed his diaper and put him in his blue snowsuit with the white fake fur around the edge of the hood. He grabbed a couple of bottles of formula and put them in the diaper bag. Once he'd shrugged into his overcoat, they left the penthouse for the limo.

As far as he was concerned, this ought to be her last day at work. His wife was a dynamo and needed to slow down. They could go get a Christmas tree in a few days after she'd had a rest. Deep in thought, it surprised him to discover they'd turned off Broadway at Seventh. It had started snowing. What was going on?

He spoke into the intercom. "Paul? Did you have to make a detour?"

"No. Your wife phoned and asked me to drop you off at the restaurant to save time. It's only a few more blocks now."

Nick frowned. "Did she sound all right to you?"

"Perfectly."

He glanced out the window, not seeing anything because Reese's call had disturbed him. Pretty soon they pulled to a stop in heavy traffic. Nick climbed out and lifted Jamie's carryall from the car seat. Paul came around and handed him the diaper bag.

When he looked around he said, "I don't see a place to eat anywhere. Are you sure you have the right address?"

"It's right there in front of you, Nick."

All he could see was a business of some kind. He brushed the flakes off his lashes. On the awning he saw the words *Chamberlain & Wainwright Brokerage.*

Suddenly he could feel the blood pounding in his ears.

His gaze darted to the front door with the same words done in gold lettering. Through the falling snow a Christmas tree with dozens of colored lights beckoned him from behind the glass.

"How long have you known about this?"

"About four months."

"You've been helping her?"

He nodded. "Driving her to and fro on her lunch hour. She gave me this." He held up his hand to show him the ring he was wearing. "There was an inscription." When he told Nick what it was, Nick felt this thickness in his throat. There was no one more exciting, more thoughtful, kind and full of surprises than his beloved wife!

"Thank you for helping her, Paul."

"It's been a pleasure. I'll be around when you need a ride home."

He started for the door.

Reese couldn't wait any longer and opened it. "Merry Christmas early, darling."

Nick came inside and shut the door, bringing the cold in with him. She held her breath, waiting to hear what he would say and think. The first thing he did was put the carryall with Jamie in it on the floor and crush her in his arms. She got a face full of snowflakes, but she didn't care.

"I don't know how you did it," his deep voice grated, "but you *did* it."

"I hope you won't be upset I put your name on the door, too, but I am a Wainwright now."

"You most definitely are, my love. If you hadn't put it on there, I'd have been devastated."

"Oh, Nick—"

Their mouths fused in rapture. They clung for a long, long time.

"Mr. Soffe gave me a bonus," she explained when he let her come up for breath. "It was enough to buy all the office equipment and furniture."

"Where did you find this place? How did you manage it?"

"When I leased the upstairs part thinking I'd be living here while I worked at Miroff's, the place was going out of business. Mr. Harvey from the bank was one of the clients I've been working with at the brokerage.

"I told him my idea for my own plans and he was willing to give me a lease and a loan to refurbish the whole place without a cosigner. That's because of you, darling. But I have to make good this time next year to pay it back. Now I'm terrified!"

Nick laughed for joy and swung her around. "Of what? I'm convinced you can do anything! Trust my wife to pull all this together."

"I used part of the money you paid me to hire Toni to do the painting."

"The waiter? You're teasing me."

"I hope you're not upset about that. He paints houses and apartments on the side part of the week to earn money while he's at night school. He attached the awning for me, too. I think he did a wonderful job."

His dark eyes roved over her face before he covered it with kisses. "I think *you're* wonderful."

"Thank you for being there for me every step of the way. I've never known such happiness in my life. Now I want to make you happy. Take off your coat and follow me upstairs."

While he removed it, she undid Jamie from the carryall. "Don't you look so cute in your snowsuit? I could eat you up. Yes, I could." She kissed his neck while she took it off. He laughed over and over again as she kissed one cheek, then the other. "I love you, little guy."

She looked up to see the love light in Nick's eyes. "Come with me."

The three of them ascended the winding steps to the studio. Reese had bought a playpen, which she'd set up next to the double bed. She lay Jamie in it and handed him a ball just his size. "With the tiny kitchen to one side of the room, there's hardly any space left to maneuver."

"I like it when we're so close nothing comes between us," Nick whispered against her neck. He slid his arms around her hips and before she knew it, they'd fallen on the bed together. "I love this innovation, Mrs. Wainwright."

"I figure it will come in handy for small naps in the next seven and a half months."

"What are you talking about?" he murmured, burying his face in her neck.

She smiled secretly. "Why, Nick Wainwright— imagine the financial prince of Park Avenue having to ask a question like that."

He lifted his head to look down at her with fire in his dark eyes. "The *what?*"

"You heard me. That's my mom's secret name for you. You *are* known to have a computer brain that catapulted you to be the former CEO of Sherborne and Wainwright. No one would believe it if you couldn't calculate the significance of a simple number like 7.5."

His black brows furrowed.

"Maybe if we go downstairs and open a few presents, you'll understand."

"Give me a hint now." He claimed her mouth again in a deep kiss that went on and on.

"Even though we won't need it until July, I got it on sale now. It goes in the limo."

More silence, and then she heard his sharp intake of breath. He sat all the way up. If she'd been worried, she didn't have to be. On his handsome face she saw the eager, tremulous look of joy, making him appear younger.

"I've made you pregnant?" he cried. "But you went on the pill."

"No, I didn't. On our honeymoon there was a night when you told me you had this dream about giving Jamie a little brother or sister right away, so he wouldn't grow up alone the way you did.

Of course you knew it wasn't possible you said and brushed it off as if it were nothing.

"After you went to sleep, I thought about it all night long and knew you were right. I grew up with siblings and can't imagine being an only child. I didn't want that for Jamie, either."

His hands cupped her face. "You've been to an ob-gyn?"

"Yes. He's one Leah recommended. I really like him. He said everything looks good."

"Reese—"

He lay back down and ran his hand over her stomach. "I can't believe you've got our baby in there."

"You're really happy about it?"

A sound escaped his throat. "What a question."

"I'm glad because I am, too. Ecstatic! We'll figure it all out."

"After taking care of Jamie, what's another one."

She laughed and rolled into him. "For the man who didn't know how to diaper a baby, you'd win the father-of-the-year award now. I sent for something special for you to celebrate. Why don't you go downstairs and get it. It's the carton with the red ribbon tied around the middle."

"I'll be right back." In a minute he'd returned.

She raised herself up on her elbow. "Go ahead and open it."

Like a little kid ripping at his Christmas present, he tore off the paper in no time. "What's this?" He lifted out the bottle. "Deer Springs Wine from Lincoln." His gaze flicked to hers. A smile lit up his face. "They produce wine in Nebraska?"

"It *is* pretty amazing. Pretty good, too. The label will tell you it comes from a hearty grape called the Edelveiss that can withstand the cold, the heat and the prairie winds."

His eyes glazed over. "That could be a description of my Nebraska nanny who withstood everything thrown at her and is now a Seventh Avenue broker to be reckoned with." He walked to the kitchen and found a supply of paper cups she'd put out. After he removed the cork, he poured himself some.

Then he walked back to the bed and sat next to her. "*Salut*, my pregnant love," he spoke in a deep velvety voice. "May our partnership last forever."

"I'll drink to that one day. I love you, Nick. To *forever*."

MILLS & BOON PUBLISH EIGHT LARGE PRINT TITLES A MONTH. THESE ARE THE TITLES FOR JUNE 2011.

— ❧ —

FLORA'S DEFIANCE
Lynne Graham

THE RELUCTANT DUKE
Carole Mortimer

THE WEDDING CHARADE
Melanie Milburne

THE DEVIL WEARS KOLOVSKY
Carol Marinelli

THE NANNY AND THE CEO
Rebecca Winters

FRIENDS TO FOREVER
Nikki Logan

THREE WEDDINGS AND A BABY
Fiona Harper

THE LAST SUMMER OF BEING SINGLE
Nina Harrington

MILLS & BOON PUBLISH EIGHT LARGE PRINT TITLES A MONTH. THESE ARE THE TITLES FOR JULY 2011.

A STORMY SPANISH SUMMER
Penny Jordan

TAMING THE LAST ST CLAIRE
Carole Mortimer

NOT A MARRYING MAN
Miranda Lee

THE FAR SIDE OF PARADISE
Robyn Donald

THE BABY SWAP MIRACLE
Caroline Anderson

EXPECTING ROYAL TWINS!
Melissa McClone

TO DANCE WITH A PRINCE
Cara Colter

MOLLY COOPER'S DREAM DATE
Barbara Hannay

Discover Pure Reading Pleasure with

Visit the Mills & Boon website for all the latest in romance

 Buy all the latest releases, backlist and eBooks

Find out more about our authors and their books

 Join our community and chat to authors and other readers

Free online reads from your favourite authors

 Win with our fantastic online competitions

Sign up for our free monthly eNewsletter

 Tell us what you think by signing up to our reader panel

Rate and review books with our star system

www.millsandboon.co.uk

Follow us at twitter.com/millsandboonuk

 Become a fan at facebook.com/romancehq